Egg-Drop Blues

Egg-Drop Blues

Jacqueline Turner Banks

Houghton Mifflin Company
Boston

Library of Congress Cataloging-in-Publication Data

Banks, Jacqueline Turner.
  Egg-drop blues / by Jacqueline Turner Banks.
    p. cm.
  Summary: Twelve-year-old Judge Jenkins has a low science grade because of his dyslexia, so he convinces his twin brother Jury to work with him in a science competition in order to earn extra credit.
  ISBN 0-395-70931-8
  [1. Brothers—Fiction. 2. Twins—Fiction. 3. Dyslexia—Fiction. 4. Schools—Fiction. 5. Afro-Americans—Fiction.]   I. Title.
PZ7.B22593Eg 1995   94-4917
[Fic]—dc20   CIP
                        AC

Printed in the United States of America
BP 10 9 8 7 6 5

I would like to thank Carol McNeal of Sacramento's Carol's Books & Things and independent booksellers across the country for their unwavering support.

To my family

· *Chapter 1* ·

If ever a guy needed a competition, I needed the Einstein Rally. I imagine when you think about something as competitive as a science fair, you think the kids are there because they're really smart, or they like to compete, or maybe their science teacher forced them to do it, but that's not why I was in it. As far as I was concerned, my life depended on that stupid competition; at least my life as I knew it.

This is how it started.

At the beginning of the new year, the second half of sixth grade, my mother had a meeting with the counselor at school, Mrs. Norville. Mrs. Norville always has an odd expression on her face, like something is pinching her from inside and she would tell you about it but she's surprised to see you. I guess my mother noticed it too because when Mrs. Keats, the mean old school secretary, took us into Mrs. Norville's office, my mother looked at Mrs. Norville and then reminded her that we had an appointment.

"Yes, Mrs. Jenkins, I remember," Mrs. Norville said, pointing to a couple of chairs.

Her expression was still that surprised look, as if she didn't know she had two chairs, or maybe she didn't know we had behinds that we used to sit.

"I asked you here to talk about Jury's situation," Mrs. Norville started.

"Judge," my mother said.

"I beg your pardon?"

"You asked me here to talk about Judge."

"Yes?"

"You said Jury," my mother told her.

"Oh, did I?"

That was when I saw her real surprised look — it wasn't much different.

"Before you came in, I had both boys' files out and I must have confused their names."

My mother nodded.

"I asked the two of you to come in to talk about Judge's situation," she said, going right back to where she left off.

I sat there for the next hour listening to my mother and Mrs. Norville talking about me like

I wasn't there and comparing me to my brother Jury.

"We're so fortunate to have a twin brother in this case to use for comparison. We can assume that, except for the learning problems, all other factors are pretty much the same for the two boys."

My mother surprised me by nodding. All other factors are pretty much the same! We're as different as any two people can be. We don't even share the same face that much anymore. My mother glanced at me when Mrs. Norville called me a "right-brain thinker." I could tell from her look that she wanted me to remember that so we could laugh at Mrs. Norville later, when we got a chance. I gave my mother a blank look. I wasn't in any mood to act silly with her; until Mrs. Norville started talking crazy, Mama had been on her side against me. Mrs. Norville handed my mother a booklet about how to deal with us right-brain thinkers, and she actually seemed grateful to get it. I hadn't been listening that much, but I could tell the conversation was coming to an end.

"Are there any other dyslexic children in Judge's class?" Mama asked while we were standing at the door.

"Learning disabilities are fairly common in every classroom across the country. I imagine we would find other kids in the school who exhibit some signs of being learning-disabled, but I can't talk about them. Our only concern right now is Jury."

"Judge."

"Yes, of course, Judge."

"Walk me to the car," she said, once we were outside. I didn't say anything, but I did start walking in the direction of the visitor's parking lot.

"That was very strange, wasn't it?"

I nodded, still wanting to show my attitude, but had to agree because she was right.

"Is she always like that?"

I shrugged.

"Did you notice how she danced around naming your reading problems dyslexia? What is wrong with calling it what it is? We aren't asking for a telethon. I'm going to phone Marilyn and ask her about it. Maybe they *have* to treat it when they give it a name."

We'd reached the van and I still hadn't said anything, but she didn't seem to notice. Marilyn is the mother of one of my best friends. My friend, Angela, is very smart and her mother is a teacher who works as the director of a community center.

"And I thought those eyebrows went out when *I* was a kid. What would make somebody shave off their eyebrows and pencil on new ones? That's just weird." She started smoothing out my collar; she always does that just before she kisses me. I tried to turn away. My mother is one strong woman, not that big, but strong. She had a grip on my neck that would have broken it if I'd try to move too fast.

She put her face close to mine and kissed me on the nose. "Whatever that attitude is about, get over it before you get home today. Don't forget your grandparents are coming to dinner." She got in the van.

I hated it when she did that. A guy should be able to have an attitude without permission.

"I love you, baby," she said as she backed out.

"Yeah, yeah," I mumbled. I could hear her laughter as the van pulled away.

Jury was standing in the hall when I got back to class.

"What'cha do?" I asked.

"I have no idea."

"Yeah, right. Miss Hoffer just put you out here for no reason."

"Not Miss Hoffer. Hennessey is in there."

I tried to peek into the classroom without being seen. He was right. Ms. Hennessey, the science resource teacher, was standing at the front of the room. She was fresh out of college and it wouldn't be unlike her to kick my brother out for no particular reason.

"Suppose Mama had walked me back to the room? It would have hurt her to find you out here."

"I've got a feeling that's what Hennessey was counting on."

He was probably right again. I wouldn't be surprised if Ms. Hennessey saw our mother as she was coming in. She pushes a cart of science stuff from room to room, and I'll bet she was going to the other sixth-grade class, which is near the counselor's office, when Mama went by. But right or not, I get tired of Jury not thinking about Mama's feelings. Imagine how she would have felt if she and Mrs. Norville had walked me back.

"What did they talk about?" he asked.

"Me."

"Duh!"

"I'm going in. I don't need this from you, too."

He grabbed my arm before I could get to the doorknob.

"Need what? What are you talking about?"

"I don't need you trying to call me stupid, too." My voice cracked, which kinda surprised me.

"Because I said 'duh'? I would have said that to anybody who answered like you just did. I'm an equal opportunity teaser — you know that."

"Yeah, okay. I'll tell you about it later."

He tried to talk me into staying out there to keep him company, but I'm not like him — I was scared of getting caught.

Ms. Hennessey jumped when I walked in the room. It was a little nervous-type jump, but I definitely saw it. I started toward Miss Hoffer's desk to put the hall pass on it and I guess Ms. Hennessey thought I was coming toward her.

"What do you want?" she asked, a little loud, I thought.

"Nothing. I just have to put the hall pass here," I answered.

When I got back to my desk, Angela had already passed me a note.

Ms. Hennessey thought you were Jury and it scared her. Can you believe that?

Angela

I looked at Angela and shrugged my shoulders. She's pretty smart, and when I don't have a clue, she usually seems to know what adults are thinking. She could be right. Maybe that's why Ms. Hennessey acts so strange with us; maybe she's afraid. But it that's true, she better forget about teaching. If the kids in a sleepy little town like Plank, Kentucky, can scare her, teaching might not be the best job for her.

I wanted to think about some of the stuff Mrs. Norville had said to my mother, but I knew I should listen to Ms. Hennessey. Ms. Hennessey is one of those kind of teachers whose test questions aren't always in the book. I learned that the hard way. We only had two tests and a quiz before Christmas and it wasn't until the second test, after I'd gotten a D on the first test, that I learned she used "other sources."

My three best friends are Tommy Maseka, Faye Benneck, and Angela Collins. With my brother, the five of us call ourselves the posse. We've been best friends forever. Tommy, Faye, and Angela are the three smartest kids in my class. I can't tell you which order of smartest they fall in, but they actually argue with each other about who's the smartest. We do a lot of things as a group, but we usually don't discuss grades or tests or anything like that. It's not that they don't discuss grades to keep from embarrassing me; they don't discuss grades because they don't have to. Usually when we have a test and the teacher passes back their A's, they stick their papers in their binders and they're ready to go on to the next thing. Jury doesn't discuss grades because he can get a C on any test just by showing up that day. He thinks grades are boring. Sometimes he really makes me mad. If he would just study a little, I know he could make grades as good as Angela, Tommy, and Faye. I don't talk about grades because I don't want to let them know how hard it is for me.

Well, after that second science test, Angela and Faye were hot, and I don't mean hot good-looking, I mean hot *mad*. Angela stormed up to the teacher's desk with her paper in her hand. That girl's not afraid of anyone. I couldn't hear what she was saying, but her mouth was moving fast. She was still mad when she went back to her seat.

At first recess that day, all three of them were standing around talking by the time I got outside.

"What did she say?" I heard Faye ask Angela. "She said some of her questions will be from outside sources." Angela said "outside sources" like it was a curse word.

"Oh," Faye and Tommy said at the same time.

"Let's go play pom-pom tackle," Jury said.

They ignored him and talked some more about the test answers.

"What does she mean by outside sources?" I asked Angela.

"She said they could be her lectures or even the science page of the newspaper."

That was when I knew I was in trouble. I tried to listen in school. It's easier for me to remember stuff I hear than stuff I read, but most teachers don't hold us responsible for it. Usually they only tell us the same things we can read in the book. I have a hard time reading. First of all, I read slower than most people I know. I can't for the life of me figure out how some people can read so fast. Just last week, I saw Faye give Angela a book that she thought was "wonderful." Angela brought it back the next day and told Faye it was so good she read it all in one sitting. I thought for sure she was lying, but then the two of them started talking about the parts they liked.

The other problem I have with reading is that I misread some words. I can read and understand technical books better than I can the stuff that's supposed to be easy. My problem with reading books that are supposedly written for kids is that they have a lot of words like "the," "and," "or," and especially "what" and "want," "this" and "that," and "not." These words con-

fuse me almost every time. There's a big differ-
ence between "oxygen not methane is in the air
we breathe" and "oxygen and methane are in the
air we breathe." At least half the time, I'll read
"not" as "and," and I'll miss not only the question
but the whole point of whatever I'm reading. I
also have problems with numbers; I turn them
around. I might read the number 879 as 798. It's
very frustrating to have this problem, but it's a
lot better knowing I have it than just thinking
I'm a big dummy. I didn't learn I had dyslexia
until last summer. I was at the community center
and I got in a conversation with Ms. Collins about
grades and stuff. I guess I started telling her
about the trouble I was having. She asked me if
I would take a test the next day.

"I'll call your mother tonight and ask her if it's
all right with her."

I really didn't want to take a test; not taking
tests is one of the good things about summer.
But I figured if Ms. Collins was going to stay
awake until after midnight to call my mother
when she got off work, then the least I could do
was take it. The test was dumb; it asked questions
like "Which number is the highest, 424 or 242?"
I remember thinking, Finally, a test I can ace.
But apparently I didn't, because Ms. Collins had
the test scored by a testing specialist. She was

fairly sure the results indicated that I'm learning-disabled, probably dyslexic. She gave my mother some stuff to read and put her in touch with the specialist. I remember my mother telling me that one theory about the cause had something to do with frequent ear infections as a child.

"If there's any truth to that it would certainly explain why you have it," she told me.

"Did I have a lot of ear infections?"

"My goodness, yes. It seems like I went back and forth with you to the doctor's every week."

"Jury didn't have any?"

"Not nearly as much. Do you remember when you had those tubes put in your ears?"

Tubes? I pictured a tube like a tube of toothpaste sticking out of my ear.

"No, I don't remember tubes."

She told me I was four when I had them inserted. Apparently they helped, because I had less ear infections after the tubes.

"So I have tubes in my ears?"

"Had. One popped out on its own and the other one was removed."

I guess it was comforting to know that I wasn't still walking around with tubes in my ears.

I tried to listen to what Ms. Hennessey was saying about the Einstein Rally, not because I thought

I'd want to be in it, but because I knew Angela, Faye, and Tommy would. I might not share their grade point averages, but I'm their friend, so I try to show some interest in the stuff they do. Ms. Hennessey was saying that the rally was being held at the Southwest Kentucky Teacher's College, which is a campus near my house that's a great place to hang out. If nothing else, I figured Jury and I would go down there and cheer on the rest of the posse. As it turned out, nothing could've been further from the truth.

· *Chapter 2* ·

I didn't give the rally or the meeting with Mrs. Norville any more thought until suppertime. My grandparents came over for dinner — they come every other Friday — and Jury brought up the rally. When I heard him mention it, I knew he was just buttering them up, or "fattening frogs for snakes," as he would say; most of his conversation centers around one cliché or another.

"It sounds like something my brother and I would really enjoy. It's time Plank had another winning team, wouldn't you say, Judge?"

He couldn't have sounded phonier if he'd spoken with a British accent. "Yes, I believe you're right, Brother," I answered. I called him brother because I know he hates it. Our mother and father have a habit of calling us both brother, especially when they're not sure which one they're addressing. My grandparents aren't stupid — they know Jury — but they seemed pleased to know that he cared enough to dream up a lie for them.

Not only could I not lie to them, I hadn't even remembered that they were coming for dinner. Maybe poor memory is another symptom of this dyslexia thing. Jury thinks I talk too much, but a lot of times the only way I can remember something is when I hear myself saying it out loud. If my mother knew I'd forgotten about the dinner, she'd say, "Didn't you see our good china on the table?" She just can't understand how I could come in the house and not notice the dining room table made up. But I can't understand how somebody *could* walk into a house and notice something like that.

"Which segment of the rally interests you, Judge?" my grandmother asked. She has a twinkle in her eye, at least that's what my daddy says. He says his mother has a way of looking at you that makes you wonder if she's laughing at you or with you.

"I have a couple of ideas about it, Grandma, but I'm going to let Jury decide . . . since he's so excited about it." I looked at Jury, like I was expecting him to make his choice right then. I could see Grandma looking at Jury out of the corner of her eye.

15

"I was planning to talk to our science resource teacher about it Monday," Jury said, grinning like an idiot. "I'm sure she'll be able to direct us."

"Your science resource teacher is the young one, right? Looks kind of like a teenager?" Mama asked.

"I wouldn't say that."

"Neither would I," I agreed. I knew Jury hated her, but he hated most of the teachers at school. I liked Ms. Hennessey all right, but she didn't look that young to me.

"She does, Ma. Looks just like one of the kids. She reminds me of how old I'm getting," Mama said.

"Nonsense," my grandfather said. He loves to point out nonsense wherever and whenever he finds it.

Jury started laughing. It always cracks him up when Grandpa says "nonsense."

"You still look like a teenager to me, Ilean," my grandmother told my mother.

I guess they know how much my mother worries about getting old. Since she broke up with her last boyfriend, she spends a lot of time in front of the mirror using skin creme and plucking chin hairs or smoothing back the gray hair in front of her ears. It's really kind of silly because, as mothers go, she's not bad-looking. She looks good for her age, but that doesn't seem to be enough.

"We missed you in church Sunday, Ilean."

"I went to Macedonia, over in Gerber. I know everybody at First already."

My grandmother made a little moan that I recognized as her "I know what you mean" moan. When both of my grandmothers are here, at some point they seem to stop talking in English. They use a kind of shorthand language, a lot of moans and grunts and raised eyebrows and words that don't mean what they're suppose to. I think it's fascinating, but Jury thinks it's boring, as apparently do my grandfathers, because Jury leaves before long and both grandfathers usually end up asleep in their chairs.

My mother and father grew up together on the same street in Plank. They always say they were like sister and brother for most of their lives. My mother told us that, before the wedding, she came to know she shouldn't marry my father, but she didn't have the heart to hurt my grandparents, both sets. It's funny to see my father and mother together now; they get along so well. If you didn't know, you would never suspect they were divorced. It's nothing like the arguing that went on before the divorce. Jury and I rarely talk about anything that happened during our fourth-grade year, the year they split up. I don't know about Jury, but all I remember is the arguing and then the silence after Daddy left. There were things that we could say that would make our mother cry, but we never knew what those things might be, so whenever she was home the house was silent.

"That's nonsense," my grandfather said, a little too loud. I think he's losing his hearing.

I don't know who said what, but Jury was dying across the table from me. I tried to kick him under the table, but it was too wide and I couldn't reach him.

"Would you like some dessert, Judge?" my mother asked.

"When doesn't he?"

"When *you* buy it or make it, *Brother*," I told him. Sometimes I have to get him off my case early or he'll start capping on me all night. My mother shot me "the look," the one that used to come before she thumped me on the head when I was younger. She'd use her middle finger and thumb and just thump, like you would if a ladybug was crawling on you. Not hard enough to hurt you or the ladybug, but it sure was embarrassing if we were out somewhere. Plus you never knew if it was going to be the look and the thump or just the look.

"Remember how close the boys used to be?" my grandmother asked nobody in particular. "I'd never seen two such loving brothers."

"That's nonsense, they always fought."

Jury had to get up he got so tickled.

My grandparents didn't stay long, even though they only live about five miles away, because Grandpa doesn't like to drive at night anymore. The bad thing about these Friday dinners is the dishes afterward. We don't have a dishwasher like the rest of the kids I know. I've asked my mother if she would get one and she says, "Why should I? I've got two already." That's supposed to be funny. I've since heard her tell somebody on the telephone that she's going to have one put in when we get the kitchen redecorated this summer.

"Do you think Grandpa might be losing his hearing?" I asked Jury as we were doing the dishes — or maybe I should say, while *I* was doing the dishes and *he* was sitting at the kitchen table watching me. I knew he was wondering why I didn't say something to him or yell upstairs to Mama, but I had my own plan.

"I don't think about stuff like that. If you think about stuff like that, the next thing you know, you'll be thinking about how old he's getting and how one day he won't be here any more and then you'll get all bummed out thinking about how there's no guarantee about any of us being here. The next thing you know, I'm walking around with a serious expression on my face and people will think I'm you!"

I took a handful of suds and tried to smash him in the face with it. He dodged and I ended up getting suds all over the curtains.

"Why don't I sign us up for the rally on Monday, save you the bother?" I said.

"You better not, unless you've got somewhere else to live."

"But Brother, didn't I hear you tell our grandparents how much you were looking forward to it?"

"This is serious business, Judge. Don't bring up that rally again in front of Mama. She'll have forgotten about it by this time next week."

I put the last dinner plate in the rack and stepped away from the sink.

"What are you doing?"

"I'm going to bed. I'll see you later." I heard him asking me about the pots and pans and drying the dishes, but I kept on walking. He knew he couldn't say it too loud because our mother would have heard and she'd be curious about what was going on. I felt no guilt. I took all the plates and stuff into the kitchen, made the water, washed everything except the pots and pans, and put them in the drying rack — he could do the rest.

By Monday, I'd forgotten all about the rally; I had other things on my mind. When I got to school, a little early so we could play a quick game of pom-pom tackle, Mrs. Norville was hunched over Miss Hoffer's desk. They were so intense, Miss Hoffer didn't even look up to say to me, "God Bless you with a good morning." Most teachers won't let you put your junk down on your desk before the first bell, but our door is always open and Miss Hoffer will always greet you with a blessing. She mumbles the "God bless you with" part so that most people think she's just saying good morning. It took us (the posse) a long time to figure out what she was really saying. When we finally figured it out we decided that she mumbles the first part so she won't get in trouble with the district for talking religious stuff to us. She's a born-again Christian. She doesn't try to sell you literature or convert you, she just seems to be happy, and you want to know why. Sometimes she'll talk to you about it if you're away from school. Last year I was at the mall with her selling candy for a school project and I asked her why she was happy all the time.

Angela and Faye had already set me up to ask. They told me that they talked to her about it one day and they thought she made God and religion sound so logical. I might talk a lot to adults, according to my brother, but I don't usually ask them about their feelings. To be honest, I had to get to be ten and catch my mother crying a few times before I even knew they had feelings. Anyway, Miss Hoffer explained a little and she did make it sound — not logical like the girls said, but real. The next time I went to church I really paid attention because, for the first time, it was real.

Monday morning, I got a gut feeling that Mrs. Norville was *not* hunched over Miss Hoffer's desk talking about the New Testament. When the bell rang, I realized Miss Hoffer and Mrs. Norville had been talking about me. Miss Hoffer was looking at me like my goldfish had just died. When it was time to read aloud, she didn't call on me but she came over and stood next to me and put her hand on my shoulder. When she did that, my heart started beating really fast. I was afraid she could hear it so I was glad when she finally started walking away. It's hard for me to read out loud, but something told me that I would have been better off trying to struggle through a few minutes of reading aloud than whatever those two women were planning for me.

I didn't have to wait long to find out what it was all about. That afternoon during science, Ms. Hennessey called everybody up to the desk, one at a time, to give us our grades. Since she has to travel around to different rooms, she can't post the grades next to our student numbers on the door, like Mr. Fritch, the phys. ed. teacher, does. There were three weeks left until the end of the trimester and we still had one big test. Her thinking was that it was best to let us know what we needed to get on the test to pass. She went in alphabetical order, so I had a chance to study the faces of the kids that came before Jenkins. I could tell I wasn't the only one in trouble, but that didn't comfort me too much when I realized that I was one of only two whose grades *my* mother cared about.

"Judge Jenkins."

I knew I was next, but for some reason I got some limited pleasure out of burying my head in my book and making her call me a second time.

"Judge Jenkins." There was attitude in her second call. I don't think Ms. Hennessey is cut out for this kind of work. Jury gave a little nod when I passed his desk. I don't know why he did it; maybe he knew I was scared. Sometimes he can be supportive when I least expect it. I glanced over at his desk. His science book was opened and standing up like a barrier and he was playing a game of dots with somebody. The look on Wayne DeVoe's face, the boy who sits in a wheelchair at a table directly behind Jury, told me that it was Wayne. I really wanted to see how they were passing the paper back and forth, but I was afraid I would bust them by staring. Both Jury and Wayne have more nerve than I believe is healthy.

"Judge, things don't look good."

No, they didn't. What was I supposed to say?

"If I had to give you a grade today, I would be hard-pressed to give you a D, even a D-minus."

"Hard-pressed" is one of those expressions I have trouble with. Does it mean it would be difficult or easy for her to give me a D? My brother uses a lot of expressions like that and it's not just annoying, it's confusing.

"What are your feelings about the trimester so far?"

"It's been difficult."

"How so?"

"I think I know what's going on and then we have a test and I end up failing it. The stuff you talk about is actually fairly easy." Why did I say that? Teachers hate it when you call their stuff easy. "But then you ask those trick questions on the tests."

"Did Mrs. Norville explain to you that they're not really trick questions?"

She saw the shock on my face. How could Mrs. Norville have explained that to me when I hadn't said anything to her about Ms. Hennessey's trick questions?

"No, ma'am." I couldn't believe I slipped and said "ma'am." I hadn't used that word in years. My father used to make us say "yes ma'am" and "yes, sir," but my mother hated it. She would tell us to stop saying it when they were still together, and she made an even bigger deal about it after he left. My father still says, "yes ma'am" to his mother.

"Sometimes when you have learning problems, questions just seem like they're trick questions."

Great. Now I had to deal with another person in the school thinking about me like I was some kind of mental cripple.

"What are we going to do?" she asked.

I glanced over at my brother. All I could see was the top of his head. He was scrunched down behind his book doing who knows what.

"Won't we get extra points for being in the

rally?" I don't know what made my mouth say the words, but after I heard them, I thought it was a pretty good idea.

"We who? I didn't know you were signed up."

"My brother was supposed to have signed up last week. Didn't he?"

We both looked over at Jury. One time he told me he had an angel on his shoulder. Sometimes I think he must because he actually appeared to be reading his book.

"Jury, will you come here please?"

I gave him the look. I know he caught it, but that didn't mean he'd be willing to cooperate.

"Jury, Judge tells me that the two of you plan to enter the Einstein Rally."

He's so cool. He didn't react, didn't even look at me.

"Is that a problem, Ms. Hennessey?" he asked. A long time ago he told me if I needed time to think about an answer I should ask a question.

"Well, no, not really, but the deadline was last Friday. I'll have to call your names in today. Which event?"

He glanced at me and I saw fire in his eyes.

"The question bowl?" she asked.

"No, the egg drop," he said.

"How many extra points will we get?" I asked, trying really hard not to look at him.

"Let's say I give you half of a letter grade for participating. That would turn a D-plus into a C-minus. If you place in the competition, I'll give you a whole letter."

"Won't the grades be in before then?"

I wasn't surprised that Jury knew that; he's good at remembering stuff. People don't think about asking him because they know he doesn't care.

"Actually, I'm supposed to turn in the grades the Friday before the rally, but I can hold yours until Monday."

"Aren't we lucky?"

Ms. Hennessey caught Jury's sarcasm, but she just smiled. I guess she was thinking she'd have the last laugh.

"Okay, Judge, you can sit down and I'll talk to your brother."

Take all the time you need, I said to myself. I sure didn't want to deal with him.

· *Chapter 3* ·

"I don't care why you did it, I don't care what you have to say to get us out of it, but you better make it happen and you better make it happen today."

He had me cornered against the wall facing the west field.

"Jury . . ."

"Jury nothing. I don't want to hear it. Just get me out of it."

"I'm going to fail without those extra points."

"You'll be dead before then."

He walked away. I tried to explain about the D-minus and the trick questions but he just started playing pom-pom tackle. He went into one of his pom-pom tackle trances and there was no talking to him.

By the end of the day, I still hadn't gotten us

out of it. I couldn't get us out of it. I needed the Einstein Rally.

If things weren't bad enough, my mother had a bright idea when I got home from school. Jury had stayed late to play a game of pom-pom tackle . . . sometimes I think he'd rather play that game than eat. Mama was home already; she was still working the morning shift at the bookbinding plant where she's an inspector.

When I walked in the door, she was sitting at the dining room table with the telephone book, a notepad, and the cordless telephone. Sometimes she can get real hyped about something somebody else wouldn't care about. During these hyper times, she'll make a lot of phone calls and piles of notes on one of her memo pads. One time, she decided she wanted to make a storage cabinet out of an old-fashioned ice box. When I got home from school that day, she had a sketch of what she was going to make drawn on her pad and she was calling all over the country trying to find an ice box for sale. Whenever I see her sitting with all her stuff at the dining room table, I know something is up.

"Hi, baby. I'm so glad you're finally home. Where's your brother?"

"He stopped to play a quick game of pom-pom tackle."

"That boy and that stupid game! Anyway, you're the person I want to talk to."

Something told me I wasn't going to share her hype. I put down my book bag and started for the kitchen.

"Just let me get a drink; I'm thirsty," I said over my shoulder.

"Hurry up."

When I came back with a soda, she didn't say anything about me drinking her sodas or my drinking "all over the house," like she usually does. Whatever she was waiting to tell me, it was really big. I hope she doesn't say Frank is back and they're going to get married, I prayed, sitting down next to her.

"Mrs. Norville called me at work. I'd asked her to check on something for me. I didn't get to talk to her — you know how my supervisor is about personal calls."

I nodded. She takes forever to tell something, but I knew from past experience there's no speeding her up.

"Shirley at the front desk gave me the message. I started to call her back during my lunch hour, but I remembered that she would — should anyway — still be at school when I got home from work, so I decided to wait."

At this point, Jury would be on the verge of screaming. He has no patience. I nodded again.

"When I finally returned her call, she told me about all the schools and programs in the area that have learning disabled classes or tutoring. Actually, I shouldn't say 'all,' because there was only one school in Plank and two programs with supplemental classes and tutoring. The other two schools are over in Gerber."

"So I'm going to take a class?"

"No. As it turns out, the classes are as expensive as the tuition."

"Tuition?"

"At Tully. Tully has a class of no more than ten kids, never more than ten, devoted to learning-disabled students."

"I'd have to go over there after school?"

"No, baby, not after school — *for* school. You'd finish up the year there. I figure the next five months is all you'd need. By the time you start junior high, you'll know what you need to do to keep up." She was grinning at me like she'd just given me the keys to a brand new car or something.

I heard Jury coming in the front door, so I waited until he was in earshot. This was something that could take his mind off killing me.

"You-want-to-send-me-to-Tully?" I asked.

"Both of you."

Jury looked first at Mama, then at me, then back at Mama.

"Both of us what?" he asked, but I know he heard.

"I found out that Tully has a program that will teach Judge how to deal with his dyslexia. I haven't talked to them yet, but I'm sure that between your father and grandparents we can afford to send you both for the rest of the year. Next September you can go on to middle school with the rest of your class."

Jury sat down suddenly, as if her words had pushed him into the chair. The look on his face was a new one for him; I couldn't read it. It was kind of like he wanted to ask her the question he's always asking me: "Are you crazy?"

"I must have missed something," he finally said.

"Okay. As I was telling Judge, Mrs. Norville called and gave me a list of schools and places that offer special classes for the learning-disabled. It turns out that I can send Judge to Tully for less than it would cost to send him to one of the after-school programs. The way I figure it, if he finishes out the year there — and it might take summer school, too — he'll be ready for junior high."

"So this is about Judge?"

I couldn't believe he asked that. I glared at him and he scowled back. Was he actually saying he'd let me go off to Tully by myself?

"I wouldn't split you up; I'm sure I can put together the money for both of you."

I could almost see Jury's mind working. I hoped he'd come up with something because, as he would say, I was drawing a blank. How do you tell somebody that you don't want to be helped? And that wasn't true at all; I really did want to learn what I could to make schoolwork easier, but I didn't want to change schools to do it.

"Everybody calls Tully a racist school," Jury said.

That was a good thing for him to come up with. Surely our mother wouldn't want to send us somewhere awful. Angela and Faye were always talking about how the kids at Tully were so stuck-up.

"Now I've thought about that. Any black person who grew up in this town knows how John M. Tully the man was. They built that school to avoid court-ordered busing. But when the residential boundaries were redrawn, each area ended up with maybe three or four black families in each school and apparently most of the racists could deal with that. The ones who couldn't went to Tully."

"And you'd want to pay good money to them?"

"Thirty years have passed, Jury. A lot of African-American and other minority kids go there now . . . okay, maybe not a lot, but surely two or three families."

"But Angela says they're the kids of university people from up north. They think our southern schools aren't good enough for their kids."

I knew that would bother her. She used to talk about the "stuck-up northern blacks" who came to the college and acted like they were too good to associate with the natives, or "townies."

"I've thought about all of this, okay? I'm willing to make the sacrifice for my kids."

Her mood was going bad fast. We'd brought up several unpleasant memories in one or two sentences.

"Mama, I talked to my science resource teacher today and she promised to give me a letter grade higher for participating in the Einstein Rally. And I believe Mrs. Norville talked to Miss Hoffer about me. You know how Miss Hoffer is. By the end of the week she will have read everything ever written about dyslexia."

She had started to speak, but I could see that something I said was working.

"That is true. If there's anything a regular classroom teacher can do to help, Miss Hoffer is the one to do it. I hadn't really thought about us doing stuff here and in your regular classroom to help."

"Especially if you'd planned to let us go to regular middle school anyway. Judge might as well learn how to do whatever it is he has to do in the real world. There are no classes of ten over at La Salle Middle School," Jury said.

"You boys go play. I'm going to call Miss Hoffer."

"You have her home telephone number?" I asked.

"Actually, I do, but I was going to try her at school. I'm glad you guys are in the rally, but it's the long term I'm thinking about." She motioned for me to get out of her way and I couldn't imagine why. When I moved, I saw that she was looking at the kitchen wall clock.

"She said for us to go outside," Jury said, giving me a look that told me he wanted to talk.

I followed him outside. He sat down on the

top step and didn't say anything for what seemed like a long time.

"What, do you just get up in the morning and try to think up ways to ruin my life?" he finally asked. His expression was serious, like he wanted me to answer.

His question hit me like a punch. Did he really believe I deliberately tried to hurt him or that I had anything to do with our mother's bright idea? If it had been night and we were having one of our "after lights out" talks, I probably would have cried. But it wasn't night, so I took the porch steps in a single leap and walked over to Tommy's.

· *Chapter 4* ·

Just as I would've predicted, Miss Hoffer promised my mother that she would do everything she could to make sure that I got all the help she could provide. She told my mother that she took a class about learning problems last fall and all the information was still fresh in her mind. Mama said she kept apologizing for not recognizing the problem herself.

"Judge is such a hard worker. I had no idea it was such a struggle for him," Miss Hoffer told her.

"When I told her I would put off sending you to Tully until summer school, she actually sounded like she wanted to thank me for giving her the opportunity to use her fall semester class notes," my mother told us over dinner the next night. She likes Miss Hoffer; what parent wouldn't? I looked at Jury. He hadn't spoken to me since my mother brought up this whole Tully thing. He looked away, as if to say, "So what; I'm still not talking to you."

"I was thinking you guys should use boiled eggs at first. I know the contest calls for raw eggs but we can wait for that."

In spite of his dislike for me, Jury looked at me for an explanation. I shrugged my shoulders. "What are you talking about?" I asked because I knew he wouldn't.

"The egg drop, silly. The way I figure it, if you use boiled eggs in the beginning, at least we can use them for egg salad and other things. There's not much we can do with raw eggs except maybe wash our hair with them."

"Ugh," both of us said.

"That is truly gross," Jury said, rolling his eyes at me like I had told him to wash his hair with a raw egg.

"Egg used to be the thing; you used to be able to buy shampoo with egg in it."

Jury and I just looked at each other. I think he was trying to lighten up. He really doesn't hold a grudge very long, not nearly as long as I can hold one, but it takes me longer to get angry.

"I picked up a copy of the rules today," Jury said.

My head jerked around. He hadn't said anything to me about getting the rules, but then again, he hadn't said anything to me about anything all day.

"Where are they?"

"In my book bag."

"Go get them."

"Now?"

"Yes, now!"

That kind of enthusiasm from her scared me. It always meant work for us.

Jury came back right away with his book bag, but it took him a while to find the booklet because his bag was jam-packed.

"Here it is," he said, his hands still in the bag. He pulled out a glossy, slick-looking pamphlet. On the cover was a multiracial bunch of, apparently, happy kids, each wearing an identical red and white T-shirt. Mama took it from his hand.

She continued eating her dinner as she read out loud. It was the first time I've ever seen her do that during dinner. She's a reader. I've seen her read just about everywhere, even during meals when she's eating alone, but never at dinner with all of us sitting there.

"Hey, this rally is a big deal. It's nationwide, like the science fair."

I looked over at Jury, but he was watching her read. Maybe he was more interested in the rally than he let on.

"This is going to be fun."

"Why do you say that, Mama?" Jury asked.

"There'll be kids there from all over. There's three in the state on the same day. Look at this." She showed us a map of the state divided in three parts. "All the applicants for southwest Kentucky will be over at the college. This sounds like so much fun."

I exchanged glances with my brother.

"It says here, 'The egg must remain uncracked when dropped from the distance of twelve feet.'"

"Twelve feet," I repeated — not because I wasn't sure I heard her, but so I would remember it.

"Okay, I know that ladder out in the garage is nine feet. I wonder what you can use as a surface?" She wasn't asking us as much as she was asking herself.

"What would you say the distance is from the patio awning to the ground?" Jury asked her.

"I don't know, but I'm pretty sure it's higher than the ladder."

"Why don't we just build something that can survive the drop from the ladder and then we can test it at school," I suggested.

They both stopped eating and reading to look at me. It wasn't that profound, but that's how they were looking. Since the meeting with Mrs. Norville, they seem to think I'm incapable of a normal thought.

"That's a good idea, Judge. What are they using at school?"

"Somebody said the top of the gym, but I don't know yet."

My mother stood with her plate. "Why don't the two of you brainstorm about the possibilities. Remember it can't cost more than a dollar-fifty to make."

Last year she went to a P.T.A.-sponsored class on helping children with their homework. The speaker talked about "brainstorming" and "first drafts." Now every time we get ready to do something we have to "brainstorm" first, and every time she reads something one of us has written she'll say, "It's a good first draft." It doesn't matter if it's your last draft or not — she expects you to redo it.

I heard her singing in the kitchen and, with all the banging around, I could tell she was doing the dishes — giving us time to "brainstorm."

Sometimes Jury has an expression on his face that makes me think he's further away than most daydreamers. A couple of times, I heard him say that he'd like to write a book, not just the world's biggest collection of expressions and clichés, but a real novel. It's the only thing he's consistently mentioned since about the fourth grade. As I looked at him, I suspected that he was somewhere far away, inside one of his plots.

"A picture would last longer."

"What?"

"Stop staring at me. What do you want?"

"We're supposed to be brainstorming," I said.

"What is there to brainstorm about? We build a better mousetrap and the world beats a path to our door." After saying that he got up and left.

He was always saying confusing things, and I wasn't sure if he'd finally slipped over the edge or if that was another cliché.

I went into the kitchen and asked my mother; she told me it was an old saying.

"It's a pretty good one, too," she added.

"Why do you say that?"

"It's your brother's way of saying he plans to win the rally."

I just nodded and went upstairs. I'm sure she had read too much into it. All it meant to me was that he didn't plan to do his part.

Things started heating up the next day. For some reason, Faye suddenly had nearly as much enthusiasm for the rally as my mother. I asked Tommy about it since he and Angela were part of Faye's question bowl group.

"I think she likes Jeff Sewell this week," he said quietly. When it comes to friends, Tommy's the best. He has a way of telling you stuff that I'm trying to copy. He just says what he wants to say; you never know how he feels about it unless you ask him. Jury says I "wear my heart on my sleeve." That's Jury's way of telling me that people always know what I'm thinking.

If Jury and Faye hadn't had a big argument about Jeff Sewell, I wouldn't have known what Faye's crush had to do with anything.

Faye asked us if she could put one of us down as the alternate for her group.

"That's cool," I said. "Use Jury's name. I don't do well under pressure. That's when my dyslexia really kicks in."

"Is that okay with you, Jury?" Faye asked.

"I'd like to know why you asked Jeff in the first place. I didn't hear Ms. Hennessey say anything about GATE teams. In fact, she made an announcement during our regular class. Am I right?" Jury said.

"Yes, but . . ."

"But what?" he interrupted. "What's up with you asking Jeff? It would be different if you went and asked somebody who's obviously smarter, but my grades are better than Jeff's. And Jeff can't talk!"

They went back and forth like that. Angela even got involved in it. Finally Angela and Tommy said that Jury could be the main selection if it meant that much to him.

It was pretty confusing. I didn't think he wanted to be in the event he was already in, much less two.

"I didn't say I wanted to be the main selection," he finally said, after everybody had joined in the argument. "I just want to know why my best friends never asked."

That really set Angela off. She accused him of jerking them around and making the rally a test of friendship. You'd have to know Angela to know that she's not a person you test.

Angela jumped up in his face and asked him if it was just some kind of test. They were nose to nose, and to some people it probably looked like they were getting ready to fight. I looked at Tommy and we both started cracking up. That started Jury and Angela laughing too. Faye ran off, which is normal for her; she can be a little too dramatic sometimes.

There were four other egg-drop groups — each was made up of kids I know and like. The really great part was that we were using the top of the multipurpose building. The building is really just one huge room. There's a stage and chairs, like an auditorium, but most of the time it's used as an extra classroom for music or a special assembly. I guess it was chosen because the top is flat.

Mr. C. (Carlisle), the vice principal, showed us how to get to the roof by pulling down a kind of ladder from the top of the storage closet. My grandparents have the same kind of setup to get into their attic. Mr. C. was nervous about letting us be up there. He spent fifteen or twenty minutes giving us a bunch of rules to follow. I noticed he looked at me and Jury a lot while he was talking, especially when he said no roughhousing. Jury didn't notice because, like the rest of us, he was looking at the dead pigeon that was laying right behind Mr. C. The roof was loaded with cool stuff like that. There were balls and Frisbees and even a dead cat. But the best thing was the view. From the roof you could see everything going on around the school and most of the neighborhood.

Miss Bailey, a student teacher, was our supervisor and she was nice. She was as interested in the dead cat and pigeon as the rest of us.

I knew things were going to be all right when

Jury came up to me and handed me a Frisbee after Mr. C. left. I threw it at a group of girls who were standing near the girls' restroom. They didn't have a clue where it came from.

"This might be okay after all," he said, as we ducked down so the girls couldn't see us.

· *Chapter 5* ·

I was hoping Jury would start to take an interest in what I was doing when it became obvious I was building our first egg container.

He didn't.

After breakfast on Saturday morning, I took the four eggs that we had left and boiled them. My mother smiled at me when she saw me getting the old pot we use to boil water and eggs. She has this theory that you shouldn't cook food in your water pot because, the way we wash dishes, she could end up with greasy instant coffee. I guess I should have felt pleased about her "good boy" smile, but I didn't. It made me feel stupid. There was my brother, the one they sometimes call the "other half," just sitting there picking at some runny yolk on the edge of his plate. I know he was humming some dumb jingle or seeing the revenge of the yolk people over the syrup patrol or something just as foolish. First he'd drag his fork through the runny yolk and then the stem of his spoon through the leftover syrup. Sometimes I'd like to be the one sitting around wasting time while he's being the "good boy."

While the eggs were boiling, I cut two pockets from the egg carton. He put his plate in the sink and then stood at the refrigerator door and drank some orange juice from the carton.

"I wish you'd stop doing that," I told him.

"I wish you'd stop talking to me." He put the carton back in the refrigerator.

"Like we want to drink your backwash in the orange juice!"

He ignored me. The next thing I heard him say was to Angela on the telephone in the other room.

"Go figure, two good months before Easter and the boy's in there playing with egg cartons."

I think Angela must have told him he should be helping me because I heard him say, "Who asked you?" That was when I figured he must have been in a really bad mood to be taking on Angela.

Although we spend more time with Tommy now, Angela used to be our best friend in the posse — in the world for that matter. Our mothers are friends and our fathers are friendly. Our fathers don't call each other or go places together, but when they're together they seem comfortable. It's kinda hard on kids when their mothers are friends because they end up telling each other all kinds of embarrassing stuff about their kids. I remember walking through the kitchen one time when I was in the third grade and hearing my mother telling Angela's mother that I had wet the bed the night before. I could have died. I couldn't think what to do, so I did the first thing that came to my mind. I ran over to my mother and hung up the telephone. She screamed because she thought something terrible must have happened to me or my brother. I screamed because I thought her scream meant that she was so mad she was about to hit me. Jury came running in from the back yard, grabbed a steak knife from the drawer, and started yelling, "Where, where?" because he thought somebody was attacking us. Then I started crying.

When my mother finally got me calmed down I told her that she couldn't tell Mrs. Collins things about us that Mrs. Collins might tell Angela. My mother tries to be what she calls "progressive," but she was raised in an old-fashioned southern black home and, I know — now — it was hard for her to accept what I was saying. She called Angela's mother back and apologized for hanging up. She wanted me to stand there and listen while she told Mrs. Collins that I had had that accident for the first time since I was a baby and she'd appreciate it if she didn't mention it to Angela. I don't know how much of our personal business is shared with Mrs. Collins, but over the years Angela hasn't been able to tease us about inside information any more than we've been able to tease her.

Angela must have made Jury feel a little guilty because the next thing he did was come back into the kitchen and ask me what I was doing.

I explained to him that I was trying to approach this egg-drop thing in a logical way. It seemed to me that egg cartons would be the best approach to take because protecting eggs were their jobs already.

"So there is a method to your madness?"

I just smiled. I didn't know if what he said was a good thing or not, but he looked pleasant enough.

"Are you going to help?" I finally asked, when it seemed he didn't have anything else to say.

"Have you ever known me to cut off my nose to spite my face?"

"No, but are you going to help?"

"Judge, you were standing right there when Hennessey told me I had to participate."

He wanted something. He was being much too agreeable. "Are you ready to start now?" I asked.

"I was thinking we'd go out and get some fresh air pushing through our lungs. Nothing like a quick workout to get the creative juices flowing."

"Quick workout?"

"Right. We'll swing around by Tommy's, get him, and then over to the park."

"For a game of pom-pom tackle?"

"Hey, if that's what you want to do, it's fine with me," he said, his voice dripping with innocence.

"Only if *I* want to?"

"All for one and one for all."

It was after three o'clock when we got back home. My mother was a little miffed because, while we were gone, she had gone upstairs and found out we hadn't cleaned our room like Jury claimed. I was disgusted with myself for taking so much time away from the project. Unlike some dyslexics, I don't have a big problem focusing on a task. If I don't have a lot of distraction, I can zone out on whatever I'm doing. My problem is shifting. If I'm distracted, it takes me a while to mentally "get back" to whatever it was I was doing. Mrs. Collins said it was a good thing that I can be so focused, but as hard as she tried, she wasn't able to help me much with the shifting thing. She gave me two fun things to do and every few minutes she would say, "switch." If I was doing the hidden picture puzzle, I was supposed to change to the easy crossword puzzle when she said "switch" and then go back to the hidden picture when she said "switch" again. It was designed to be hard for me, and it was. The first time I was supposed to switch, I just sat there looking at my pencil. It was like I'd forgotten what it was for. I had to start silently talking to myself: Okay, now you're working a crossword puzzle, so look at the next clue three down, "the part of a plant that is in the ground." Suddenly the words "plant" and "ground" had no meaning. I had to think about each word. I'd just barely written in the word "root" when Mrs. Collins said "switch" again and I was looking at the alien pencil in my hand.

Looking at the egg carton and the scissors on the kitchen table reminded me of that day with the alien pencil; it was like looking at something a Martian left behind. All I could think about was running across the park's field and laughing when a boy named Ray-Ray slid across the line on his knees, making two big rips in his pants. I stared at the egg cartons. I knew my original idea was floating around somewhere in my head, but I just couldn't catch it.

Jury came in and sat down. He was still grinning, still happy about the silly game.

"Jury, did I tell you what I was going to do with the egg carton?"

"Nope."

"You have no idea?"

"None."

I sat down too. We both looked at the egg carton.

"I was thinking," Jury started, "why don't we get one of those plastic eggs that Mama's pantyhose comes in, fill it up with confetti — a whole pound of which I just happen to have under my bed — and drop it from the ladder?"

"You have a whole pound of confetti?"

"Yup, a whole pound." He eased back in his chair with his hands clasped behind his head. He looked very pleased with himself, like he was the only one who thought to squirrel away valuable confetti before the coming of the worldwide confetti shortage.

"Why, Brother?"

"Stop with that 'brother' stuff. I bought the

confetti just before Ayreal left. I was going to throw it around at the going-away party. You know how I was always sarcastic with her. I was going to pretend that I was happy she was moving to California."

Ayreal was a girl who went to school with us for a few months at the first of the year. She and my brother really had a thing going. Even now he looked sad when he said her name.

"Why didn't you do it?"

"I thought about it and I figured I better not do anything that could be misinterpreted. I didn't want her to think about it later and decide that I actually was happy."

"You really did like that girl, didn't you?"

"I sat down here to talk about your stupid egg drop!"

The real Jury was back. "Okay, that sounds good. I think it's kind of what I had in mind to do with the egg carton. Maybe we're twining."

Twining is something my mother likes to talk about. It's like when we all go our separate ways at the mall and Jury and I come back with the same thing, bought at different stores. When we were little, our father would take one of us while Mama took the other to buy our Christmas gifts. Then we would meet up and switch parents and buy a gift for that parent. At least twice we bought them the same thing.

"I'll go get the confetti, Einstein."

"Hey, I asked you not to do that."

"This is the last time I'm going to say it. I don't think you're dumb, stupid, or any of that. If you ask me, I don't even think you have a learning disability. I just think you try too hard. I am not going to stop calling you names related to intelligence because it hurts your feelings. To thy own self be true."

He went to get the plastic egg and the confetti.

I smiled. He doesn't think I have a learning disability. He said it was the last time he was going to tell me, but as best I can remember, it was the first. So when he calls me stupid he means it the same way he means it when he calls the rest of the posse members stupid. I sat back in my chair with my hands clasped behind my head.

· *Chapter 6* ·

Monday was a very strange day, even for me. It all started at first recess. The bell had rung and we were all coming back from the west field and a good game of pom-pom tackle. Tommy rounded the corner and ran smack into Mr. C., who was standing by the water fountains. Everybody started laughing because Tommy did a pratfall, like running into Mr. C. had knocked him out. Tommy can fall better than anybody I know. He's great to have on a baseball team because whenever the ball gets a little too close, Tommy grabs his arm or chest and falls and, of course, he gets to walk to first. He got real hurt a couple of months ago during a game of pom-pom tackle and, that time, it took me a few seconds to realize it wasn't just one of his pranks.

"That's enough of that, young man," Mr. C. told Tommy, which, of course, made us all laugh even harder. The group had started walking away when Mr. C. called Jury's name. Jury stepped up to him and Mr. C. nudged even closer.

"Don't think I don't know what you boys have been up to out on that west field. If I catch any of you playing pom-pom tackle between now and the Einstein Rally, I'm putting you on suspension, and suspended kids can't participate in extracurricular activities."

"Why are you telling *me*?"

We were all shocked. Jury was almost shouting, and he's not a back-talker at school — our parents wouldn't stand for that.

"I beg your pardon?" Apparently Mr. C. thought he was smarting off, too.

Much calmer, Jury said, "I'm not saying anybody was playing the game, but if somebody was it would have to be more than one person, so why are you only saying it to me?"

"I know who the leaders are."

We continued on to class, but the rest of the day everybody teased Jury, calling him "fearless leader" and bowing to him — stuff like that.

At lunch Angela and Faye got in on it. Somebody told them what had happened and they both were, in the words of Angela, "incensed." Faye wanted to do something, like start a petition or send around the word that everybody should be late to class after first recess on Tuesday.

"My mother says the reason students don't get any respect in the nineties is because they don't demand it," Faye told us.

"Yeah, but what would she say if you got kicked out of school because of a protest?" Tommy asked.

"Actually, I think she might consider it my finest moment so far."

Everybody was really impressed that Faye's mom was like that, but that wasn't going to help me and Jury if we got kicked out. I noticed Angela was quieter than usual. She likes the sound of her voice too much to ever be completely silent, but she didn't have as much to say as you'd expect. Lunch was almost over before I realized what was up with her. Mr. C. is her friend; she really likes the guy. I asked her about it on the way to class.

"That's very observant of you. I do feel torn." Angela, typically, was being dramatic. "He's always gone out of his way to be nice to me."

"Yeah, but you've known Jury longer."

"Oh, there's no contest, Judge. I want to be part of whatever action we plan."

God, I wish I could talk like Angela.

Jury didn't want anybody to "do" anything.

"We'll just have to be even more careful not to get caught playing," was all he said.

I was worried. This wasn't just about him getting kicked out of school. My grade depended on us being in that stupid rally, being in the rally depended on us staying out of trouble, and us staying at Faber depended on all of it.

"It's not just about you," I told him.

"I know that."

"Act like you know it."

"What do you want me to do?"

"We have to stop playing the game for the next two weeks," I told him.

"Why do you always have to take things to the extreme? We don't have to quit playing, we just can't get *caught*."

"Why aren't you getting this!" I shouted.

Jury put his hand on my shoulder. "Just chill. It'll be okay."

I went on with whatever I was doing, but I thought about it the rest of the school day. I'd rather argue with Jury and know what he plans to do than just sit back and let it happen. I don't think he has enough fear. Fear keeps you from doing stupid stuff.

The next strange thing happened when we got to the roof for egg-drop practice. I'd put the containers we made at home up there before school. Ms. Hennessey told us to do that so they wouldn't get broken during the day. We didn't have to bring eggs; the school provided them. When we got to the roof, Randall Gifford and Dan Brungardt were already up there with a few other people.

Randall ran up to Jury. "Do you still want that bet, Jenkins?" he asked.

"Yeah. Why, did you get some kind of great inspiration over the weekend?"

"I don't need great inspiration to beat you. Let's double the bet."

They shook hands.

"What was that about?" I asked.

"I bet them that we'll place higher than they will."

"How much?"

"Was five, now it's ten."

We walked over to the corner table where I had stored our stuff. The student teacher was standing by the table and she had something in her hand, holding it like it stunk or something. As I got closer, I could see that it was the container we had made from the pantyhose egg. It was smashed in a trillion pieces.

Jury groaned from the pit of his stomach. I saw him drop his book bag and sprint toward Randall and Dan. I don't know how I knew what he was about to do; we must have been twining again. I grabbed him by the shoulders and we locked in mid-flight.

"Let me go! I'm going to kill them!"

"Don't, Brother. We'll get kicked out."

"You just stay out of it."

"I can't, you know that." There was no way I could just stand by and watch my brother fight two guys. Not to mention my mother would kill me when she found out about it. She was always telling us, "You two take care of yourselves and each other."

Miss Bailey ran over and grabbed Jury's arm. I let go of him. My father told me a story once about a fight he got in when he was a kid and one of his older brothers held his arms, trying to stop him from fighting. His brother ended up giving the other guy a chance to hit my dad with a couple of good sucker punches.

"Jury, somebody climbed up here and destroyed *all* of the containers," she said, loud enough for all of us to hear.

I looked over at Randall and Dan, then I tapped Jury on the shoulder. Randall was holding something that looked like a broken-up mudball.

"I guess they got them, too."

"I guess."

When we got home from school, there was a package for me on the porch. My mother was working mandatory overtime so it had been outside since around noon. We have one of those mailboxes that is really just a slot next to the front door. It's a good way to get your mail because you don't have to get dressed on Saturday morning when your mom tells you to go get it, but packages and sometimes magazines end up on the porch. It's not that I'd expect some hardened criminal to steal off our porch — it's not that kind of neighborhood. I just can't help but wonder if Jury's cassettes from his music club wouldn't be tempting to some kid passing by.

Maybe I'm a worrier, like my brother says.

I spotted the package first because I ran home. It's still cold out. We didn't have much of a winter as far as snow and freezing rain goes, but it's been cold enough to see your breath. And I *hate* cold weather. Cold weather means football and football means conversations about football games. Although now I know why I have such a hard time following football games on television, it's still very confusing. One team has the ball, they do something, the other team does something else, and at the same time the announcer guys are talking about what the guy with the ball did while he was still in college. I can watch it in person, but if I have to watch it on television I have to turn the sound off.

I knew the package was from my father as soon as I saw the handwriting on it. My mother and father have penmanship that's easy to spot. My mother prints everything, and my father has big curlicue writing that I usually associate with girls. In fact, all he'd need to do is dot his *i*'s with a heart and it would look just like some schoolgirl sent me something.

Jury hovered like a hawk while I ripped off the grocery bag paper.

"It's a tape recorder! This is so bogus!" Fast-reading Jury read the box and was making his comments before I knew what was happening.

"Look, he sent an article." I scanned it. It was something some doctor at the University of Michigan had written about "helping the learning-disabled child." My father had underlined a part that mentioned buying the kid a tape recorder. That was as close to writing a note as he gets. He lives in Nashville, but we still see him just about every other weekend and we talk to him about three times a week.

Jury took the article from my hand. "Check this out; Daddy underlined it. It says kids who remember better by hearing should read and record their text chapters and play them back later. I guess he thinks you should do it too." We went inside.

Jury took the recorder out of my hand and took it over to the kitchen table. "This isn't fair. I've been asking for a CD player and they both keep saying, 'Why, you don't have any CD's,' and then you get this for failing a test. I wish somebody would tell them it doesn't make sense to buy any CD's if you don't have anything to play them on."

I started laughing. Then he played my laughter back for me on the machine and we both cracked up.

· *Chapter 7* ·

The next couple of days were pretty quiet. Everybody in our class was worried about the big science test on Friday. Even the brains — Tommy, Faye, and Angela — were talking about studying for it. I'd been reading a chapter or two into the recorder each night. It was fun the first night, but by Tuesday it was just another way to do something that was boring, plus Jury was complaining that he was learning more than he wanted to know because I played my chapters back at bedtime.

"There's such a thing as overlearning," he kept saying. I'm beginning to think he says stuff like that so he won't be disappointed if he doesn't do well, or as he says, "to cushion the blow." Jury cares about grades more than he lets on. I've seen the look on his face when he gets a C and he was expecting something better. The sad part about his act is that he's the reason he gets C's. I know the only reason he got average grades last year was because he set the teacher up to believe that he was an average student. I think teachers get a mindset and then they keep giving that grade no matter what you deserve. Our fifth-grade teacher was like that; she took a lot of shortcuts. She was the first teacher who tried to separate us.

"When I was a child they always separated twins," she told our mother at back-to-school night. "I'm going to talk to the principal about getting them placed in different rooms."

"Why?" my mother asked.

"I don't understand why they're still together. They should have been separated before now."

"Why?" my mother asked again. I could tell she was starting a slow burn. My mother doesn't half-step at anything. She plays hard, and when she gets angry, she gets really angry. I was hoping our teacher would say something logical before Mama blew it. From my own experience, I know that "just because" is something my mother hates to hear.

"It's always been done that way, so I'm sure educators have a good reason for it."

"What?"

"Well, I don't know. Why don't I research and let you know?"

"Fine. I'll be doing my own research, too."

The next day, when we got home from school, she had the dining room table loaded with library books.

"I found it!" she announced when we walked in the door.

"Good for you," Jury said, on his way to the kitchen. That was as much as he planned to say.

"What did you find?" I asked.

"I've been looking for something to explain why it's good to separate twins. Well, actually, I was trying to find something to justify not separating you."

I sat down. She looked like she was about to deliver a long explanation.

"Since they've always done it, there isn't much information to support it or refute it. But I did find a study done on year-round students. Since they go year-round, siblings and sometimes cousins have to be in the same room so they can be on the same track."

"Track?"

"So they'll have the same vacation time. I'd imagine it's really important to plan for your babysitters and family vacations."

I nodded.

"This study says there was an improvement in grades when siblings were in the same room, even when cousins and close family friends were together."

"Makes sense to me. Sometimes when I don't get something in class, I'll ask Jury when we get home. Sometimes I can just look at him during class and he'll help me get the answer." I was talking too much again. I could see she was getting too interested in what I was saying.

"How, baby?"

"Oh, sometimes I'll look at him and he'll point to the book, then I'll know that the answer is in the book. Sometimes he'll turn the book around so I can see the page that it's on. Sometimes he'll just shake his head no."

"What does that mean?"

"It can mean that it's a trick question and nobody knows the answer or it can mean that it's a stupid question and it's not worthy of an answer or it could just mean that he doesn't know."

"I think you two should stay together, don't you?"

"Definitely."

Later that day I caught heck from Jury about what I told our mother.

"What'd you blab about now?" he asked me after dinner.

"What do you mean?"

"Mama just cornered me and started slobbering all over me, mumbling something about me being a good brother. I'm not her brother — the path leads to you!"

He's still a good brother, but he's a lousy egg-drop partner. We had to start over from scratch. I didn't take the notes I was supposed to, so I had no idea how much tape I had wrapped around the egg after I put the bubble packing (the kind people like to pop) around it. The egg cracked the first six times we tried it.

"I don't care if I never see another egg salad sandwich," Jury complained when he saw me carefully gathering up the cracked eggs to take home to Mama. The other kids were probably starting to feel the same way. When Ms. Bailey saw us using boiled eggs, she asked about it and we told her what my mother had suggested. She thought it was a good idea, so she told the rest of the groups to boil their eggs and take the rejects home. Like us, the other groups are using the raw eggs to test a container that had already passed the first couple of drops. Even though the school was providing eggs, we used so many that we had to bring some from home, too.

"You fetch today," I told Jury when we got to the roof on Thursday. I was tired of wrapping the eggs and going down to check them after the drop. Jury did seem to enjoy the actual drop, but who wouldn't?

"Why me?"

"I'm tired of doing all the work."

"Like it was my idea to be in this stupid rally."

"Okay, it wasn't your idea. I've got that. Does it mean I have to carry the whole thing?"

"Quit whining. I'll go get the stupid eggs, but I'm not staying past the late math class today!" At our school we have an early math class that starts at 8:00 and then the other half of the class comes at 9:00 and stays an hour for late math. They had to do this when the school became overcrowded. Angela, Tommy, and Faye are in the GATE class, which meets at 8:00, so they have to have late math. We're in early math, but for most of the school year now, we've figured out reasons to still be at school when they get out of late math.

"Fine."

"I know it's fine." He started walking in the direction of the ladder.

Before he got to the ladder, Mr. C. came on the roof. "So you're up here," he said.

"Who, me?" Jury asked, which was kind of odd because Mr. C. was looking straight at him.

I stepped closer. That man was holding my grade, and ultimately my future, in his hands. If he was getting ready to suspend my brother for some reason, I wanted to hear all the details.

"What's this about, Mr. C.?" I asked, surprising even myself.

"How long have you been up here?" he asked me.

"We came together," I said, nodding at Jury. I didn't know how he'd have answered the question, but I was pretty sure that this time I hadn't messed up.

"Why?" I asked again.

"I just sent a little boy to the hospital with his mother. He probably has a broken arm. I'm fairly certain he was playing your silly game."

"Wow — who was he?" we said in unison.

"That's not important right now. I just want to know if you know anything about the game."

"We were up here," I said.

"You can't get me on this one, Mr. C.," Jury said in a kidding way. I almost thought he was going to slap Mr. C. on the back. Mr. C. blinked at Jury, and I could tell he was holding back a smile.

"While I'm up here, you might as well show me how your project is coming along."

The Mr. C. that Angela swears by was with us for the next fifteen minutes. He walked around and looked at everybody's containers. He asked a couple of us if we had any idea who might have vandalized the projects. Just before he left, he said to Jury and me, "Keep up the good work, boys."

"I thought he'd never leave. It might be too late for me to get in on the next game."

"What?" I asked my brain-dead brother.

"You know how it is when somebody gets hurt. We just pick up the game and move it to a new location."

"Excuse me, earth to planet Jury! Was I with a Jury pod-person when Mr. C. came, fully prepared to kick you out if you hadn't been able to prove you were up here?"

"And don't think I'm not more than a little annoyed that somebody organized a game without me."

Jury was having a conversation, but it wasn't with me. He shoved all of his junk into his backpack, and without so much as a "see you later" was off looking for a game.

· *Chapter 8* ·

Thursday night was serious study time for us. Mama cleaned up the kitchen after hearing Jury's little speech, which she called a tirade: "This is a conspiracy. The best shows on television always come on on Thursday night, the one night that everybody knows is reserved to study for the stupid Friday test." He goes through it at least once a month.

"I'll do the dishes tonight," she said, interrupting Jury. "You guys go study."

I went upstairs to study at our desk. I don't know what our parents were thinking about when they bought only one desk. But it turned out okay; I don't believe I've ever seen Jury studying there. When he studies upstairs, he usually sits on his bed, but most of the time he studies in front of the television. Angela says we're lucky that Mama'll let us do that; Mrs. Collins won't let Angela. My mother says she was a fairly good student and she studied in front of the television, so she doesn't sweat us.

The night went fast. I reread the five chapters that made up the unit and listened to the tape while I was going to sleep. In fact, I must have fallen asleep because I don't remember turning it off.

It seemed like I was asleep for about an hour when I heard Jury's alarm. Since he got his new alarm clock-radio for Christmas, I'm up as soon as I hear the music turn on. Otherwise, I have an early morning attitude because I get angry listening to him hit the snooze bar over and over again.

I was dressed and finished with breakfast by the time Jury came downstairs. He's definitely not a morning person, but neither am I. One thing we agree on, we leave each other alone in the morning. Our mother leaves soon after Jury's alarm. She's a morning person. Since she started her latest diet, she exercises to a video in the morning. It uses a lot of old music from her generation and that's what I have to deal with if I come down too early.

By the time I got downstairs on test day, she was gone. She left us a note on the refrigerator: "Good Luck on the test!! Love, Mama." She likes exclamation points. I thought the note was nice of her.

"How lame can you get?" Jury asked when he came down and saw the note. But he doesn't fool me.

I've got the best teacher in the world. Right after the bell for the late math kids rang, Miss Hoffer made an announcement. "I know everybody is a little concerned about their science test today. Instead of social studies, why don't you take out your library books or your journal, whichever you prefer. If you haven't studied, and I know all of you have, you can study for the test, but I'd prefer to see you doing something more relaxing."

Jury's hand shot up.

"No, Jury, you cannot talk or play games in here or outside. You can read or you can write in your journal." Everybody started laughing. Even Jury laughed, so that must have been what he was going to ask.

I'm rereading one of my favorite books, *Bunnicula* by Deborah and James Howe. It's the first chapter book I ever finished. I've read it once each year since the first time I read it at the end of fourth grade. Plus, I think it's a really funny story.

I was lost in the story when I heard Ms. Hennessey's voice. I don't know how long she'd been in the room, but Miss Hoffer hadn't left yet so I figured it wasn't very long. They were talking about something really quiet. Just before Miss Hoffer took her grade book and left the room, I heard her tell Ms. Hennessey, "I'll pray for her; it'll be all right." She touched Ms. Hennessey's arm lightly. I couldn't help but wonder if somebody in Ms. Hennessey's family was sick.

Ms. Hennessey asked Faye to pass out the papers. As Faye walked by she gave me a quick pat on the back. I must have been looking pretty scared.

I eyed the test. It was three pages long, handwritten. I hate when teachers don't type their tests. Most of them have pretty decent writing, but it's confusing enough without adding handwriting to the problem.

I didn't look up again until Ms. Hennessey said, "Okay guys, put down your pencils."

It was funny. I felt like I was floating or in a time warp or something. The light in the room even looked brighter.

"That was quick, wasn't it?" Ms. Hennessey asked the class. I think she was being sarcastic, but to me it did feel quick. Most of the kids moaned or mumbled under their breath. Ms. Hennessey laughed.

But in spite of the time warp problem, I was sure I'd passed. It was a new feeling. Sometimes I'd hear Tommy, Faye, and Angela talking about tests: "I aced it," they would tell each other. I always envied their confidence, but now I was having that same feeling. It was — what — kind of scary?

During the test, I did some things my mother and Mrs. Norville showed me. At one point when the question didn't make any sense, I turned the test paper upside down and read it that way. It forces you to see each word. I talked to myself quite a bit, too. I'd say things like, "Okay, Judge, why don't you eliminate the answers that don't work." One of the multiple choice questions was: "The formation of sedimentary rocks is closely associated with ____." The choices were: a) water, b) lava, c) sand and d) chemicals. I asked myself, "What is the definition of sedimentary rock?" Of the four choices, only water came up in the definition. I asked myself a few more questions, and again, only water came up in the answer. I chose water. The whole thing took all of two or three seconds, and for all I know that could be the way normal people think anyway, but it was new for me. Over time, facts have proven to be unreliable for me — at test time, all of a sudden I didn't know the stuff I thought I knew. I was sure about an answer only when the question was almost identical to the fact as I learned it. In other words, the only way I could have been sure about my water answer was if the question was asked using the definition I learned.

"How'cha do?" Jury asked during the first recess.

"I actually think I did all right."

"Yeah, it wasn't as hard as I expected. I think your stupid recording helped."

"Is that a thank you?"

"Would a rose by any other name smell as sweet?"

"What?"

Instead of explaining, he ran off to start a game.

After our last class, we went to the roof and I got some good news — our container finally survived three drops in a row. We're using the plastic egg container, wrapped in three layers of bubble wrap and then jam-packed with Jury's confetti. An engineer from the air force came to speak to us about impact and aerodynamics. Miss Bailey was concerned that we were losing sight of the science aspect of the egg drop. Actually, the engineer's lecture was all right. On the walk home that day, I pictured myself in an air force uniform teaching kids how to gauge the force of an impact. It was something I would not have imagined prior to my feeling confident that I passed my science test.

Every other Friday night is our eat-out night. It used to be on Saturday, but that day was crowded with other stuff. Sometimes we eat in and have pizzas delivered. When my mother was still dating her old (in actual years) boyfriend Frank, he managed to convince her that eating out two or three days a month was too expensive for a single mom. I know she's lonely and she worries that she's too fat to meet another boyfriend, but I sure am glad Frank is out of our lives.

My mother wasn't home when we got home, which was strange. She's not that crazy about her job. She'll usually turn down overtime on a Friday.

Jury wandered in about twenty minutes after I got home.

"Where's Mama?" he asked.

"It's not my day to watch her."

"Ha-ha, you slay me. Now answer the question."

"I don't know, okay?"

He actually grabbed the remote, which I had

picked up when I heard him coming up the steps, out of my hand and changed the channel.

"Uh, excuse me!"

"I just want to check something out."

"On the news?"

He sat down on the sofa, crowding out my feet, which were there first.

"Yeah, on the news. I heard that some TV cameras were filming some of the Einstein Rally groups."

"Which ones? Don't tell me, the question bowl?"

"Surprisingly enough, it was the dramatic interpretation group."

"Who told you?"

"Angela. Angela was hot. She said if any honor comes to Faber out of this thing, it'll be her group that brings it, not some stupid bunch of fourth- and fifth-graders acting out the murder of Julius Caesar."

"She's probably right," I said.

"I know. It's disgusting, isn't it."

I nodded and we sat in silence waiting to see if the kids from Faber would show up on the news. During the last five minutes there was a quick shot of the dramatic group and then a longer closeup of a little red-haired girl from the fifth grade. Everybody thinks this kid is really cute, but she reminds me of that movie with the redheaded doll that killed people. The biggest part of the spot was a closeup interview with Ms. Hennessey. The way the announcer was grinning all over himself made me see Hennessey differently. He was acting like she was cute or something.

Our mother was coming through the doorway with an armful of groceries; Jury didn't move.

"Here, let *me* help you with those, Mama."

"Aren't we lucky to have him around, Mama?"

"Listen, I'm going to tell the two of you right now, I don't have the patience for any stupid stuff tonight — okay?" She flopped down on the spot I vacated. I put the bags away.

"Okay, now both of you come give me a hug and tell me how the science test went today," she said as she kicked off her shoes.

· *Chapter 9* ·

I think the rally took on another level of importance when I learned that our mother was late on Friday because, in addition to stopping by the grocery store, she had put in two hours of overtime for the woman who was working for her on the Saturday of the Einstein Rally — next Saturday. Mama usually has to work one Saturday per month.

"I've already told Ms. Hennessey that I'll drive a carload over in the van," she explained.

"Wouldn't that be a vanload?" Jury said.

"Don't push me, Brother," she warned, but I could see she was kidding him.

I'll never understand why so much of Jury's foolishness walks when it comes to adults.

"Too bad your daddy chose this weekend to come up."

"He'd probably change it if we ask," I said. Jury gave me the look.

"You mean you haven't asked him?"

"We didn't want to bother him; it's no big deal," Jury said.

"Maybe not to you, but we care about these things."

Jury told me later that he was afraid asking Daddy would just add to the pressure.

"I thought you said it was no big deal?"

"It isn't, but you know how they get. They'll turn it into a big deal."

Well, to me it was already big. In seven days, the knot in the pit of my stomach that I was beginning to feel every time I climbed the ladder to the roof would be a thing of the past.

My father tries to be a part of whatever is going on with us. Sometimes we don't tell him about something happening during the week because we don't want him to face the two-hour drive at night. During soccer season at least three of our games are on weekdays, but we don't mention them. He hates to miss one of our games, but with them being in the fall when it gets dark earlier, we just don't tell him so we don't have to worry.

Everybody on our team, the Warriors, knows when one of our parents is missing because the sideline volume is cut by half. Both of them are very competitive and they make excellent cheerleaders.

The kids on the question bowl team were getting together over at Tommy's to practice. Even though Jury's name is on the list as an alternate, he hasn't said anything about going over there. But for that matter, he hasn't made any of their daily after-late-math practices either.

"Are you going over to Tommy's?" I asked after dinner.

"Naw, I'm sick and tired of hearing about the Einstein Rally. I'll be glad when it's over."

Finally we agreed on something!

Our father called early Saturday morning. I'm a hard sleeper and I didn't hear Mama's call to come to the phone. But I heard some of Jury's end of the conversation. It seems to bother him that I can sleep so good. He could have taken the telephone just about anywhere upstairs — it has a super-long cord — but he chose to sit on the edge of his bed, speaking as loud as he would on the pom-pom tackle field.

"Okay, Daddy, we'll be ready . . . Okay, bye," I heard him say.

"Ready for what?" I asked.

Jury jumped, like I startled him. He turned around.

"We need to get a bell for you to wear around your neck."

"What?" It wasn't even nine and he was already saying strange things.

"Like the cat."

"What cat?"

"Never mind. Daddy's going to be here in about a half hour; he's taking us to breakfast."

"Mama too?"

"No, just us. He said there's something he wants to talk to us about."

"Did he give any hints?"

"Not a one. But he sounded up."

As Jury was talking, he was moving toward the bathroom. I think he thought I was going to race him for the shower. He could have saved his energy; I was still sleepy. He went in the bathroom and I leaned back on my pillow. I wasn't hungry; it was definitely one of those rare days I'd choose sleep over food.

I looked at the bedroom paint job we did last summer. I could see one or two spots where the paint was uneven, but for the most part, I was proud of it. My mother decided she wanted the whole house painted. She was going to call my uncles, Daddy's brothers, but we talked her into paying us to do it. My uncle Jerry did come over and show us how to tape up the wood trimming and brought us some tarps to protect the carpet. It turned out to be easy and kind of fun. Even Jury had to admit it was easy.

"We're setting a dangerous precedent," he kept saying. "Precedent" was one of our fifth-grade spelling words. Our teacher used the phrase "dangerous precedent" in one of the sentences she said during the test, and Jury had been using the phrase ever since.

"Why do you keep saying that?" I finally asked.

"If we let her know we can do this, she's going to expect more out of us."

"So?"

"This year she pays us, next year we do it because we should be 'committed to our house looking good.'" The 'committed to the house looking good' phrase was one my mother always used when she told us to clean up. I knew Jury was right, but what could we do about it? Actually, I agreed with her; I do want the house to look good.

She paid us three hundred dollars. We were able to spend fifty dollars apiece on whatever we wanted, but we had to put the rest in the bank for our Disney World trip this summer.

Jury can take some of the fastest showers — my mother always asks me if I've used soap, but she asks Jury if he ever uses water.

"I betcha Daddy's getting ready to move back up here."

"I doubt it," I said.

"What do you think this is about?"

"I don't know, but isn't it supposed to be my job to worry about stuff?"

"I'm not worried; I just don't like surprises."

I waited to see what he was taking out of the closet to wear before I went in to take my shower. I hate it when I decide to wear something and it turns out to be the same thing Jury is wearing — surprisingly, it happens pretty often. I was safe; he was wearing his signature outfit, a black T-shirt and black overalls. He wears it so often it's a wonder there's any dye left in that combination.

My father was already at our house by the time I got out of the shower. Nobody knocked on the door or came to get me, so I guess waiting was no big deal. I was surprised when I came downstairs and found his girfriend sitting next to him on the sofa. They were drinking coffee with my mother and all of them were laughing about something Jury had said.

I tried my hardest to remember the girlfriend's

name. Didn't it have something to do with a flower? Rose, Iris, Lilac — is that a name? Maybe it wasn't a flower, maybe it was a fruit . . . no; banana wasn't a name!

"Here he is. Judge, you remember Lilly, don't you?"

I tried to answer like Jury would. "Yes, I remember Lilly." I walked toward her with my hand out. I noticed the raised eyebrow my mother gave my father. Jury laughed.

· *Chapter 10* ·

Breakfast out wasn't a unique idea this Saturday. The lines were out the door at the first two places we tried, so we ended up at the Smorgasbord at the mall. It's actually one of my favorite places to eat because you can get what you want, but most people don't think about it unless they're already in the mall. There was even a line there, but only about fifteen people were ahead of us.

My father and Lilly were beginning to make me sick. It was bad enough that she sat so close to him in the car that, from behind, he looked like a two-headed man. But she held his hand in line and kept looking at him like he was saying something fascinating, something that would save the world. Most of the time he wasn't even talking. Dad wasn't making matters any better; at one point I saw him kiss her on the neck and then, when it was time for us to move up a little, he kind of "pushed" her forward by patting her on the behind. I know he didn't know I saw it, but I did and I wanted to scream, "Now cut that out!" I know she just turned thirty, but doesn't he know how old *he* is? As usual, Jury seemed to be completely self-absorbed. He seemed to be more interested in what I was putting on my plate than the fact that Lilly and our dad waited until the last possible moment, when they reached the trays and stuff, to let go of each other's hands.

At least he waited until we were all sitting before he made his big announcement. Jury put his tray down and then said he was going to get some milk.

"I'll wait until you get back to say what I'm going to say," Daddy said, as a way to get Jury to hurry.

"Duh."

Lilly thought that was hilarious.

"Don't laugh at him. I told him to stop saying that last time I was up." But our dad had that grin on his face as he said it. Once again Jury was getting away with something.

He came back, put his milk down, and then sat. "Okay, let's hear it."

"Thank you for your permission." Dad reached over and took Lilly's hand again.

Jeez.

"As you both know, Lilly and I have been seeing each other for . . . what?" He looked at her.

"Over a year," she said.

"That's right, over a year. A couple of days ago, I asked Lilly to be my wife and she agreed."

I looked at Jury and he looked at me like he was confused or maybe he missed some of what Daddy was saying. Maybe he was still thinking Daddy had come to make an announcement about moving back up here.

"It's not . . . I mean you two don't . . ." He looked at me. "Help me, Judge."

I would have helped Jury, but I didn't know what he was trying to say. We all just stared at him.

"Okay, I'll just say it."

But he didn't just say anything. He took a drink of milk. He made it look good like in a commercial. I was tempted to go get some too, but I wanted to hear what he was going to say, exactly how deep he planned to put his foot in his mouth.

"Should we expect an addition to our family soon?" he finally blurted out.

Our father looked at me like he wanted me to explain. I shrugged.

"Jury, son, that's what marriage is, the addition of a wife or husband to one's family." Lilly giggled.

"Daddy, I'm asking is she expecting?"

I could almost see the little wheels turning in my father's head, rolling around over the word "expecting." Expecting, now what does that mean?

"You're asking me if Lilly is pregnant?"

At first he looked pleased with himself for figuring out his number-one-son's riddle, but almost immediately behind that came an angry expression. Jury didn't make matters any better by saying what he said next.

"Duh. I mean yes. That is what I was asking."

This time Lilly's giggle was a little nervous-sounding.

"Well, just for future reference, that's not the proper question to ask when somebody announces his or her engagement. You tell the man congratulations and you wish the woman a happy life or you tell her she'll be a beautiful bride or something like that."

I would have pointed out that his thinking could possibly be politically incorrect. Our mother is trying to raise us not to be chauvinistic, which my father calls a bunch of garbage, but it didn't seem like the time to bring it up.

"And no, Lilly is not pregnant. We're getting

married because we want to spend the rest of our lives together."

If love could make a person fly, Lilly would have flown out the restaurant when my daddy said that.

I couldn't cope. I forced myself to think about the Einstein Rally. What was I going to wear next weekend?

"Well, say something, Judge," Daddy said.

"Okay. Congratulations, Daddy, and Lilly, you're going to be a beautiful bride."

She'd have to be a beautiful bride — she looked like a younger, slimmer version of my mother. I've heard my grandmother Jenkins talking on the telephone to her friends and she'll describe somebody as, "a pretty brown-skinned girl like my daughter-in-law Ilean." Skin shades are a big deal in my father's family, but I haven't figured out why yet. I wonder if Grandma will still call my mother her daughter-in-law after Daddy remarries?

Jury excused himself to go to the restroom.

When Jury finally came back, my father made a few lame attempts to get us to say something about how we felt about them getting married, but neither of us were biting. Finally Lilly kicked him under the table and he stopped trying to get us to talk about it.

All things considered, breakfast was pleasant enough. It's hard to mess up breakfast food for me. It's just the opposite for Jury; he hates breakfast. After he came back from the restroom he didn't eat any more, and he'd only eaten a few mouthfuls before he left. I was pretty sure he threw up while he was in there. I know his sick-to-the-stomach look.

After the announcement, things were a little strained. Daddy promised to call us later in the evening so just the three of us could get together to go bowling. He used to ask our mother along for stuff like that, but I guess those days are over. I love to watch them compete; they both play hard.

Jury and I stood outside and waved good-bye to Daddy and Lilly. "Are you okay?" I asked Jury as we walked up the porch steps.

"Except for my insides being twisted in knots, I guess so. Did that come out of the blue for you too? Or was it just me?"

"I suspected it was something like that — marriage, living together, engaged. It's all the same." I sat down on the top step and he sat next to me.

"He and Mama will never get back together."

"I never expected that."

"But didn't you hope it?"

"No. I like them better apart. Have you forgotten how it was just before they separated?"

"No, I remember. But I figure they've grown up a lot since then. It seems to me that if you just wait these things out they get better. Look at Grandma and Grandpa Jenkins; they don't even talk much to each other anymore, but they seem happy."

I didn't have anything to say to make him feel better. I would have sat longer, but it occurred to me that our mother hadn't come to the door. Usually, when we go somewhere with our dad, she's right there with a lot of questions when we get home. She always pretends that she's just showing her motherly interest, but it's more than that. She still cares about everything Daddy does.

I decided to go see how she was taking it. There was no doubt in my mind that she knew, either by instinct or because my father had told her already.

What I saw when I opened the door made me laugh so hard Jury came in from where he was sitting. Our mother had brought her stationary bike down from her bedroom and she was pumping away while watching a cooking show on television. She was wearing a silver sweatsuit-type thing I'd never seen before and there was a green avocado mask on her face.

"Come on, it's not that funny," she said between puffs.

When I got closer I could see her eyes were red, and I wondered if she'd been crying.

"I decided if I moved it down here, I could use it while I'm wasting so much time watching television every night with you guys."

"I beg your pardon; that's the quality time everybody talks about."

She threw a towel at Jury and he seemed all right again. She climbed off her bike.

"If either of you want to talk I'm here."

So she knew.

"I've got a headache; do you have anything?" Jury asked.

That was probably the third time in my life that he's said anything about having a headache.

"Go get my purse, Brother."

I looked in the usual places for her purse and found it on the kitchen table. She dug around until she found a tin of tablets and gave Jury two.

"Why don't you go lie down."

I didn't like the sound of that; it would mean all of the Saturday chores would fall on me.

"Do you want me to take your books back to

96

the library for you?" I asked Jury. Our books weren't due for another couple of weeks, but better the library than cleaning.

Luckily, I caught Mama off guard. She actually thought it was nice of me to offer to take Jury's books back with mine.

"Maybe I'll read up on something I can use next weekend while I'm there."

"Okay, baby." She kissed me at the door. I felt terrible; I do have a conscience.

The library is about six blocks from our house, so I rode my bike. I'm not part of the Saturday crowd, but I saw a few people I knew and each of them felt the need to tell me that Faye and Angela had just left. I guess that's the trouble with being part of a group; everybody expects you to always be together. I went over to the magazines and grabbed a handful of good ones, then I settled down in one of the big comfortable chairs.

A couple of hours later when I got home, our father called to say he wasn't going to be able to take us bowling. One of my uncles was having a little get-together for some of my father's old friends to meet Lilly. He invited us, but I think he was relieved when Jury said he didn't want to party with a bunch of old people. We would have been the only kids there. When he hung up, Jury mumbled something about his head still hurting.

Sunday we all went to church — we go about once or twice a month. My mother told us early in the week that we were going this Sunday because we hadn't been all month. Lilly and my father were there, sitting right next to my Grandparents Jenkins, which is on the same pew that my Grandparents Reynolds, my mother's parents, sit on. Usually we sit with them or right behind them. My mother sat on the opposite side of the church. It was my first time ever sitting over there.

My mother wore the dress she bought for her company's Christmas party. Also, she wore a little more makeup than usual. She looked really pretty. After church almost everybody told her how nice she looked. I think it started to have the opposite effect before long. I think she heard, 'You're not as young, pretty, or slim as Lilly, but you look nice, too.'

"Let's get out of here," she whispered to us at some point. It's a really friendly church — after service they have coffee and doughnuts in the basement. It's the only part I look forward to, but I was with her about leaving. I knew it was just a matter of time before one of the grands asked us how we felt about Daddy's announcement.

We ended up eating big ice cream sundaes at a place that advertises the "best ice cream this side of the Mississippi." When we got home our mother asked me to move the stationary bike back to her room.

· *Chapter 11* ·

The week before the rally was probably my most intense week ever. Jury summed it up pretty well on Friday when he said, "The one week I needed a pom-pom tackle game every day, twice a day, and I've only had time to play once."

After school on Friday we had a going-away party for Miss Bailey. Her student teacher's term was up and she was going back to teacher's college. She kept apologizing about not being able to be with us on Saturday, but we understood. She'd made reservations to fly back to Michigan during her term break before she knew anything about being our Einstein Rally adviser.

"I'm glad your mother is doing better," I heard Miss Bailey say to Ms. Hennessey as she was gathering up her junk to leave.

"Thanks. I hope I wasn't too hard to be

around. Her condition has really been on my mind a lot."

That explained things. It explained why Miss Hoffer was offering to pray for Ms. Hennessey and it explained why her mind always seemed to be elsewhere and her attitude wasn't the best. If my mother was really sick, I wouldn't be the nicest guy to be around either. I made a mental note to tell the posse.

Our grandparents Jenkins took us out to dinner on Friday night. We went to a steak house that my grandpa likes. It was okay, but I'm not really a steak person; I'll take a hamburger over it any day. It seemed like my grandmother was gushing over Mama a lot. I guess my mother saw it too because at some point in the evening Mama reached across the table and took Grandma's hand.

"Ma, I loved you before you were my mother-in-law; I'll always love you. I'm happy for Rus and Lilly. Do you know what I'm saying?"

Grandma nodded. I kind of wish she hadn't known what my mother was saying because I needed further explanation.

The grands didn't come in after dinner. We went in and got in our usual positions for television. Within what seemed like seconds after sitting down, my mother was fast asleep.

"I don't know why she even bothers to sit there," Jury commented when she started snoring.

"I guess it's not that unusual; Angela and Faye both said their parents fall asleep as soon as they sit down, too."

"You'll talk to people about anything, won't you?"

I didn't answer him. Just because he wants to play the strong silent type doesn't mean I shouldn't talk to my friends. I left him in front of the set at eleven when the news came on. Watching television and denying that we had a big day ahead of us wasn't going to make it any easier.

The next day started off like any school day, which wouldn't be unusual except it was Saturday. Our mother called us at 6:30, only today she didn't leave soon after her wake-up call. And this morning we didn't ignore her call to wait for the alarm. We showered, dressed, ate breakfast, and were ready to go without mentioning the rally and without anybody asking anybody else if they were excited or nervous. I do know when not to talk.

I was glad the whole posse decided to ride over to the campus with us. My mother was complaining in a playful way about the gas it took to pick up Tommy, Faye, and Angela.

"Next time we'll just have them meet us at our house," I suggested.

"No. By the time they walk over here, they might as well walk to the campus," she said.

The entrance of Southwest Kentucky Teachers College is only about three blocks from our house, but the campus is huge. It's built across two different rolling hills.

"So what you're saying is you should go pick them up?"

She swatted at Jury, but he ducked out of her way before she could make contact.

We picked up everybody and they were all going through a quiet thing, too. After everybody said their good mornings, we all just stared out the windows and rode. We weren't sure if we were supposed to go over to the school first or not, so we did, since we had time to spare. Ms. Hennessey and a couple of parents were there with the kids who needed rides. They followed us over in a caravan.

Almost as soon as the van went through the big green gates, I knew it was going to be a special day.

"Feel the electricity in the air," Faye said as

103

her feet touched the ground. She started twirling around like the good witch had just zapped the ruby slippers back on her feet.

Like I said before, Faye and Angela can be quite dramatic. But I had to agree with her this time. A band from somewhere deep in the campus was playing some marching-type music. Every time the drum beat, I could feel it inside like it was my heart. For some reason, I thought about how athletes must feel during the opening ceremonies of the Olympics. There were all kinds of kids there, wearing all kinds of T-shirts. Angela and Faye had had a big argument last week about Angela going to the student council and getting them to buy matching T-shirts for all the Einstein Rally participants from Faber.

"We're going to look so lame, so babyish," Faye complained.

I don't know how Angela was able to call this one — sometimes I think the girl is psychic — but nearly everybody had on matching school T-shirts or hats or both. One school even had matching jackets.

Most of the kids seemed to be carrying something like cars made from shoe boxes or weird-looking stuff like mobiles made out of vegetables or spools of thread; one kid even had some animals shaped out of what looked like dryer lint.

"Check out all the babes," Jury *thought* he whispered. Like I needed him to tell me. Angela and Faye gave him the "you pig" look, but I know they were checking out the dudes — and there were probably twice as many guys.

Tommy and Jeff, the boys on the question bowl team, had moved ahead of the Faber group. I guess they were acting as our scouts. If the red-and-white T-shirts Angela picked out weren't so visible, they might have gotten lost in the maze of people. They stopped just before they got to the registration table. We caught up to look at something that was so cool I immediately developed a new appreciation for science.

There was a square section of lawn about as big as half a football field blocked off by yellow plastic police department crime scene tape. It stretched away from the crowd over grass that had been covered with some kind of white stuff that looked like salt. Inside, where the tape was about waist-high and held up by caution signs all the way around, were ten lawn-mower-powered cars being driven by kids who didn't look much older than us.

"This is my event next year," Tommy said. I didn't have to ask to know that all the guys agreed with him. The kids in the cars wore helmets and some kind of padded suits, but they were on the far end of the square moving faster than I would have expected any lawn mower to go. I could have stood there watching that all day, but the adults caught up and Ms. Hennessey told us we better go register before we got too fascinated by anything else.

It's a good thing Ms. Hennessey told us to move on. When we got to the registration table, we learned that the question bowl was scheduled for 9:45, less than fifteen minutes away. Our event was at 11:15, just ten minutes after the scheduled end of the question bowl event. That seemed like enough time to get from the LS&A (literature, science, and arts) building to the physical education building. The campus is getting smaller as I get older, but it still seems huge to me. I've taken summer recreation classes in the phys. ed. building and Angela's father's office is in the LS&A building, so I know the campus as well as I know my back yard. When Ms. Hennessey asked, "Does anybody know where the LS&A building is?" all five of the posse members pointed at a building up the hill behind her head.

"Somebody in group A — that's the sixth-graders — has to wear this and somebody in group B has to wear this," Ms. Hennessey announced as she held up two pins that said "captain" on them. Every hand in the B group shot up. All of us sixth-graders just looked at the B group and shook our heads. You would think that by fourth and fifth grade, they'd know better than to volunteer for something without knowing what they were volunteering *for*.

"What does the captain do?" Tommy asked.

"Yeah, besides wear that stupid pin," Jury mumbled.

Ms. Hennessey jerked her head around to see who'd said it, but she didn't catch him. I would think by now she'd know who to suspect.

"I imagine they'll be asked to introduce the members of the team. What else could be involved?" she answered.

Tommy went behind Faye and forced her arm up. She started laughing, so I guess Ms. Hennessey figured it was okay to hand Faye the pin.

"I'm going to get you for that," Faye threatened Tommy.

"Oh, you know it's your deepest fantasy to wear a pin like that every day of your life," Tommy told her.

Jury gave Tommy a high-five.

We all started walking up the hill en route to the first event. Everybody was quiet on the walk up; things became serious again. I was hoping the question bowl would go fast so the egg drop would be over sooner. I was actually looking forward to Sunday, even though our mother said we had to go to church again. I looked over at her. She was walking directly behind Jury holding on to his shoulder. She always talks about being out of shape, but she wasn't winded at all and I was.

We got to the top of the hill. The A team was meeting in the auditorium on the first floor and the B team was in the second floor auditorium. Ms. Hennessey went with the fourth- and fifth-graders. My mother and two other adults went with the rest of us.

The auditorium was about as large as a small movie theater. There were eight tables on the stage with a button and light bulb in front of each of the chairs behind the tables.

This part of the rally was between Tully, Kennedy, and Faber from the jump. I think all of the other five teams were able to answer at least one question each, but that was about all. For the next hour and twenty minutes, the Faber team was neck and neck with the other two. The questions were unbelievable. Even if I live to be a hundred, I don't know how I'd ever know some of that stuff. They asked questions like, "What is the largest organ in the body?" Why would anybody but a doctor know that? Faye answered it right when she said the skin. Now if ever I've heard a trick question, *that* was one. Who would think of the skin being an organ? If I wasn't hyped enough, the intensity of the question bowl left me feeling like my heart was going to exit my chest.

But I was on the Southwest Teacher's College campus that Saturday morning for the egg drop.

The last twenty seconds of the question bowl were played in slow motion. I remember Angela screaming and all of a sudden Jury hugging me, then he started running toward the back of the auditorium. Although I started running behind him, at that moment I had no idea why.

"Jury, wait!" I called out.

"We've only got seven minutes to get there," he said over his shoulder, but he didn't stop.

I'd become so wrapped up in Tommy, Angela, and Faye's event that I'd lost track of the time. I followed Jury out of the LS&A building, down the hill, and onto the bike path that led to the phys. ed. building. It was a shortcut we discovered when we were little kids. I only saw one or two bikes on it; I think most of the foot traffic was Einstein Rally kids. I looked back to see if I could see my mother and the rest of them. They were about half a block behind.

I never would have guessed the setup they'd

planned. The phys. ed. building is flat like our multipurpose building, so I figured we'd be on top of the roof, but I soon learned there was more to it than that.

As soon as we got close to the building I spotted some of the other egg-drop groups waving us over. All day I'd seen college-age kids walking around with neon-orange vests on over whatever they were wearing. I didn't think much of it; I figured they were doing some kind of work. It turned out they were guides. Dan and Randall were talking to a girl wearing one of the vests. Jury was standing next to them.

"Over here, Brother," he called out.

For him to call me brother in public, I figured he must really be nervous. I got in line beside him and tried to catch my breath.

The college girl with the vest was holding a clipboard and making notes on it. She came to Jury just as I got to him.

"Name and school?" she asked Jury.

"Yes," he said. That's one of his old tired lines.

"What is your name?" she asked, never looking up. She was kind of cute. She had long straight blond hair down to her waist.

"We're Judge and Jury Jenkins from Faber."

Now she looked up. "What's with you Faber

kids? First I get Randy and Danny and now I have Judge and Jury?"

"Kids?" we both said. She wasn't twenty-one yet either.

"Come on, guys, what're your names?"

"We really are Judge and Jury Jenkins from Faber."

"Well, that's what I'm putting down here. You have less than a minute to get up on the roof. The containers you sent over should be there."

We followed the rest of the kids and adults into the building and climbed the regular stairs instead of a ladder up to the roof.

It was even cooler up there than it was from the roof on the multipurpose building. I could see the whole campus. All the different colored T-shirts and flags the schools had brought made the grounds look like a field of wild flowers.

"May I have your attention, please." The speaker was a young woman with a portable mike. "This is the Division A Egg Drop of the Einstein Rally. If there is anybody here who is supposed to be with the Division B Egg Droppers, please see one of the guides now."

Of course there were a few kids who made surprised sounds and ran up to one of the guides or made a dash for the stairs. Everybody laughed. I looked down at the posse. Angela and Faye were standing on either side of my mother talking with enough enthusiasm to worry me. Tommy saw me looking at them and he gave me a thumbs-up.

There were four yellow lines painted on the rooftop about four feet apart, labeled one, two, three, and four. A sign next to lane three listed Faber as one of the schools for that lane.

Up to that point, it hadn't really interested me to look and see if all seven of our containers made it over intact, because I saw that Jury went right over to them when we got to the roof. Now I went over to where he was standing with Randall and Dan and the rest. When I got close enough, I could see that he and Randall were having another one of their big arguments. Those two are too much alike.

"Do you have any money?" Jury asked me.

"A dollar and twenty-three cents. Why?"

"If you had any money I'd make big-mouth Randall put his money where his mouth is."

"And you want to use my money to put with your mouth? Forget it. You'll already owe him ten dollars if we don't place better than them. And Mama wouldn't like the idea of you betting."

"Then it's a good thing she won't be finding

out about it, isn't it?" He knew he didn't have to wait for an answer before he went on to something else. "I wonder what those two girls down there are talking to her about."

"Yeah, so do I. But I'm more worried about what Mama's telling them."

"Whoa; I hadn't even thought about that angle."

The next announcement made everybody get quiet.

"Will the first four teams step forward."

Faber wasn't in the first four. The announcer asked all students not in the first set to either watch from below or understand that they would not be able to see the drops from the roof. I only saw five or six kids run toward the stairs.

There were wooden "guides" built on the edge of the roof in front of the four lanes. At about the level of my waist was a sort of armrest that each kid used for the arm that was going to drop the egg, so everybody's egg was released at exactly the same height.

Being a little taller than the average kid my age, I could see over the crowd as each kid was handed an egg from a large container that was on a small table. I watched as they took the egg and carefully placed it in the container they built. Each team got two tries.

113

"At the sound of the bell, drop your first egg," the announcer said.

The bell sounded and in what felt like seconds, I heard cheers and ohs.

"With the sound of the bell, drop your second egg."

Now I was more conscious of the time, and it seemed to take a little longer before I heard the cheers and the ohs.

Two schools were eliminated because neither one of their eggs survived. One school had one egg survive and the other school had both survive. The school team whose egg survived both drops was told to get out of the lane; they were automatically in the semifinals. The school was Tully.

The school that had one egg survive stayed where they were and three more schools filled in the remaining lanes. According to the rules, the new schools had two chances, while the other school had just one chance to continue with the next group or be eliminated.

"At the sound of the bell, drop your eggs."

This time only one egg survived; it belonged to Morgan, a school from Bowling Green, which was as far east as our rally went.

On the second try, the Bowling Green school joined Tully on the sidelines and one team got to stay in the lanes. The school that got to stay was in lane three so we had to wait.

"Are they trying to kill me?" Jury whispered. I knew he was talking about us waiting out another round. I nodded.

I couldn't see the reaction of the people down below because there were guides all the way around to keep kids from leaning over trying to see the contest. I'm sure it was a safety precaution. But I was thinking about the reaction of the crowd, because I knew that — until they actually saw the contest — most of them would've thought it was easy to build a container that could survive the drop. Until we tried to do it I thought it would've been easy, too.

It was finally time for the first Faber team; two girls we didn't know. None of them survived the first drop. At the sound of the second bell, all of them survived. Everybody thought that was funny. The next trial, only one survived and it wasn't the Faber team. Everybody crowded around to let them know we felt badly too. Randall and Dan were next, and their first egg didn't make it. Their second egg did, and that slowed it down once again for us.

"At the sound of the bell, drop your eggs."

I was surprised when I realized I was holding my breath and crossing my fingers for Randall and Dan. When we heard the cheers and ohs, we had no idea who they were for. I knew when I saw Randall and Dan leave the lane and the sad looks on their faces that their egg didn't make it. Everybody crowded around them, as they had the first team. I wasn't at all surprised when I saw Jury hug Randall and tell him he was sorry, but I'll bet Randall was.

"Good luck," Randall said as we got in the lane.

Jury and I had already worked out how we were going to do it. He was going to pack and drop the first egg and I was going to pack and drop the second.

I was close enough now to see the crowd below. My mother was up front so she could see the whole thing.

"At the sound of the bell, drop your eggs."

Our confetti-filled, bubble-wrapped egg container seemed to fall in slow motion. I watched the reaction of my mother as the college students opened the containers. When she started jumping up and down and cheering, I didn't have to wait to see the guide hold up the intact egg. Suddenly my eye caught another woman a little farther back in the crowd. I noticed her for two reasons: she seemed really happy when the eggs went up in the air, and she was African-

American. Jury had been the only African-American participant in the four lanes.

"That's Lilly!" we both said at the same time. Apparently she'd caught his attention, too.

"There he is!" Jury said as he pointed to our father standing behind and to the right of my mother, which was about two rows ahead of Lilly.

It was time for me to get in the lane.

I hadn't been conscious of the band music since we left the registration area, but it seemed like they started playing again to accompany me. Again I heard the drums beating with my heart. I felt awkward, like my left hand had been switched with my right. As I packed the container, I wondered what would happen if I broke the egg trying to get it into the container — would that count?

"At the sound of the bell, drop your eggs."

The egg drop was actually more of a letting go than a drop. To me, dropping seems to involve a pushing off, and I didn't push off, I just opened my hand and prayed. Again, I looked at my mother. Jury screamed, "Yes!" into my ear at the same moment I saw my mother jump into the air. She reminded me of Michael Jordan's hang time; she seemed to freeze mid-jump.

The other Faber teams congratulated us as the

guides moved us over to the side with Tully and Bowling Green.

For the next thirty minutes, we waited while the rest of the schools went through their drops. When it was over, there were five schools who had survived two drops.

Up until that point, I hadn't paid much attention to the way the wooden guide was built. I was surprised when I saw the college kid pull the guide up another foot or so. Next, they cleared the crowd out of the way to move another wooden platform up next to the first one. I couldn't figure out how it was going to work.

"Oh," a few students said when one of the officials tested the standing platform and the new height of the armrest. The announcer requested that the first four teams return and stand on the new platform. This time we had two drops each.

"At the sound of the bell, drop your eggs."

Jury dropped the egg, and I waited for our mother's reaction. She cheered; I cheered; we all cheered. Two teams had broken eggs.

Then it was my turn.

This time, everything went much smoother, even though the new height felt a little strange.

"At the sound of the bell, drop your eggs."

I dropped it with my eyes closed. When I

opened them, Lilly was the first face I could find. She was cheering. I breathed again.

Jury and I stepped aside with Kennedy. When it was over, Tully was the only other team that had survived both drops. It was down to the three of us.

"Now what?" Jury wondered. We didn't have to wait long. The guide was moved up another level, and wooden boxes were added to the platform in the first three lanes.

Jury stepped up on a box and loaded the next to last container. It seemed like enough time hadn't passed by when I saw the disappointment on my mother's face.

"It's up to you," Jury said.

"No matter what, we've got third place," I said.

"Hey, that's right." He gave me a high-five.

I went through the drill and dropped the egg. I just wanted it over.

This time I looked at our dad. He and my mother embraced. All three of us survived the drop. I didn't realize it was over until I heard the ding-ding-ding of the final bell.

"Don't we have to drop it again?" I asked Jury.

"No, this is where those essays that we wrote come in. They'll decide who's first and second by their essay scores."

I wanted to say something else, but at that moment all of the kids up there from our school were crowding around us and patting us on the back and stuff.

The announcer kept repeating that we were to "evacuate the roof." I guess he was afraid all those happy parents and friends were going to rush the roof.

We went down. Mom, Dad, and Lilly rushed up to hug us. It was great. As far as I was concerned, I didn't need the awards ceremony to feel wonderful.

"I guess I owe you this?" Randall said to Jury, stepping in between our parents. He handed the ten dollar bill to Jury.

When Randall walked away, my dad asked, "What was that about?"

Jury looked at me. For the first time in a while my brother was at a loss for words.

"Would you believe it's part of an awards pot?" Jury asked.

Me and Lilly were the only two who laughed.